"There are no guarantees in romance, Priscilla."

"I'm not into taking risks," she replied.

"Oh, really? Is that why you jump onto the roofs of burning buildings?"

"I knew you were going to bring that up," she said with a laugh. "That's different. If you understand fire, you can try to predict what it will do. It follows the laws of physics. A guy, on the other hand, doesn't follow any rules—of physics, logic, anything."

"Guys are easy," Roark scoffed. "Give them food, sex and football on a regular basis and don't take away the remote control."

He got a smile out of her with that, but she didn't seem inclined to continue the debate.

Roark's needs were even simpler. He wanted Priscilla back. In his life and in his bed. But he sensed that now wasn't the time to push. He had to give her some time to figure out that she wanted him as much as he wanted her.

He couldn't resist one last attempt to convince her. "I'm not really that complicated. What you see is what you get. And your secrets, whatever they are, couldn't possibly be that bad. I consider it a personal challenge to figure you out."

She opened her mouth to protest, but he planted a quick but firm kiss on her lips.

Dear Reader,

I've admired women who choose to pursue a
traditional "man's" career, whether that be as a cop,
a soldier or a construction worker. So of course
I couldn't resist including a female firefighter at
Fire Station 59. While I was doing research for this
series, I discovered that firefighting may be *the* last
place where women are accepted. Most of the male
firefighters I interviewed did not want to work with
women. Period.

So, in addition to the usual hurdles a rookie faces, my
heroine, Priscilla, has challenges simply because of
her sex. Then there's the gorgeous arson investigator,
further upsetting her equilibrium, and a matchmaking
mama dragging her to distraction. I admit, Priscilla
is my favorite of the firefighters, with her tough-girl
attitude masking a few deep-seated insecurities.

I hope she is a heroine you can root for, too!

All my best,

Kara Lennox

An Honorable Man
KARA LENNOX

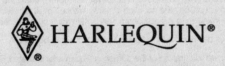

HARLEQUIN®

TORONTO • NEW YORK • LONDON
AMSTERDAM • PARIS • SYDNEY • HAMBURG
STOCKHOLM • ATHENS • TOKYO • MILAN • MADRID
PRAGUE • WARSAW • BUDAPEST • AUCKLAND

ISBN-13: 978-0-373-75158-7
ISBN-10:   0-373-75158-3

AN HONORABLE MAN

ABOUT THE AUTHOR

Texas native Kara Lennox has earned her living at various times as an art director, typesetter, textbook editor and reporter. She's worked in a boutique, a health club and an ad agency. She's been an antiques dealer and even a blackjack dealer. But no work has made her happier than writing romance novels. She has written more than fifty books.

When not writing, Kara indulges in an ever-changing array of hobbies. Her latest passions are bird-watching and long-distance bicycling. She loves to hear from readers; you can visit her Web page at www.karalennox.com.

Books by Kara Lennox

HARLEQUIN AMERICAN ROMANCE

Many thanks to the guys at Station 14 for helping me with firefighting details: Lieutenant Charlie Salazar, Firefighter Ken Sutcliffe, Firefighter Joe Hinojosa and Firefighter Byron Temple.

Chapter One

The alarm sounded, and rookie firefighter Priscilla Garner cocked her head and listened. Maybe it wouldn't be for her crew—but she hoped it was.

"That's us!" someone called out.

A fire at last. Priscilla was more than glad to halt the endless chopping of onions, her current assigned task. Captain Campeon had finally stopped putting her in charge of meals at Fire Station 59, because though she honestly tried, the end results usually were inedible.

So she got to do the fun stuff. Like chopping onions and peeling potatoes. Sometimes she felt as if she was in the Army pulling KP duty. And if she wasn't chopping or peeling, she was likely mopping, scrubbing toilets or washing dishes. Such mundane tasks made her twenty-four-hour shift creep by.

It would have been easy to assume she was being picked on because she was the only woman at the station, but she knew better. Her best friends, Ethan and Tony, got pretty much the same treatment. Such was the life of a rookie.

Otis Granger, suddenly alert, turned off the meat he'd

been browning for chili and they headed wordlessly to their stations and struggled into their turnout gear.

As a rookie Priscilla's job was to stick close to Otis, watch and learn. He was twenty years her senior, a hulking man with a huge belly and skin the color of milk chocolate. At first he had fought like a cornered feral cat about having to work with a woman. But once he'd realized she was determined to succeed at her job, he'd let up. They'd actually become friends.

Priscilla vaulted into her spot on the jump-seat, next to Ethan. She finished bunking out, fastening Velcro cuffs as the engine, with its siren blaring, headed for what had been reported as a Dumpster fire behind a Chinese restaurant.

The engine hurtled through Oak Cliff, a large, diverse section of Dallas south of the Trinity River. As they sped down Jefferson Street, the main shopping drag, past colorful stucco shopping centers, kids on bikes stopped to gawk.

Drawing nearer to the fire, Priscilla saw a plume of heavy black smoke rising up in an otherwise flawless October sky, and when they turned the last corner she realized they'd be battling something more serious than a trash fire. A storage shed behind an apartment building was burning fiercely.

Lieutenant Murphy "Murph" McCrae, their driver, reported the change in conditions over the radio to the dispatcher as he tried to get the engine down the narrow alley. But the passageway was constricted by a Dumpster that was off its base.

"We'll have to go around to that parking lot," he announced. "Garner, Granger, go on foot. Looks like there's a chain-link fence needs taking down."

Priscilla was on it at once. She jumped down from the

engine, grabbed a pair of bolt cutters, and in forty pounds of gear ran as fast as she could toward the blaze. She pulled her self-contained breathing apparatus over her face as she ran. The small building was completely engulfed, and the trees nearby were smoldering and starting to catch.

Damn, this was exciting!

Feeling the heat of the fire on her face, she went to work on the fence. Moments later, Otis was at her side, steadying the hot metal with his insulated gloves and pulling it aside as she cut each link. Bystanders began to gather, and she had to chase a few of them back. By the time the fence was dispatched, the engine was pulling up in the parking lot adjacent to them.

Priscilla was itching to stretch hose and attack this beast. Another siren wailed in the distance, indicating a second engine was on its way. She and Otis unfurled the main hose, while McCrae worked the various controls, and soon they had a fully charged line with which to attack the flames.

It always amazed Priscilla how quickly a fierce, hot blaze could be tamed. In a matter of minutes, the fire was under control. The burning trees were extinguished, the charred roof and walls of the shed had been soaked, first with water, then with foam.

"Garner!" Murph bellowed. "I want you and Granger on the roof."

She hopped to obey. Man, she loved this, tearing holes with her pike pole and looking for hot spots, which Ethan promptly extinguished from below. *Ha, take that. And that!* No flickering ember would escape her clear eye or her sharp pike.

They hadn't been called to a real fire in over a week.

And since Priscilla still had months left on her paramedic training, she didn't usually get put on medical emergencies, so she'd been bored and antsy.

She tore at the blackened composite shingles, giving the roof savage stabs.

Shouted conversations drifted around her until one specific word caught her attention: *arson.*

She paused. "Ethan, did someone say it's arson?"

"Yeah, there's a bunch of paint cans and rags piled next to an outside wall. Probably just malicious mischief."

A few seconds later Murph called Priscilla down from the roof.

Any mention of arson made Dallas firefighters jumpy these days. A huge fire the previous spring, when Priscilla was still at the fire academy, had proved lethal for three veteran firefighters because the arsonist had rigged the roof of the burning warehouse to collapse. The fatalities—the first in many years—had sent shock waves through the department. The loss had been especially hard on her firehouse, Station 59, where the men had all worked.

But the arsonist hadn't stopped there. He continued to set fires every few weeks and he was setting them more often as time progressed.

When a familiar black Suburban pulled into the parking lot, Priscilla tensed. Captain Roark Epperson. He'd been an arson instructor at the fire academy; he'd also taken a much more personal interest in Priscilla, though no one else knew that.

Since their brief, explosive fling had ended uncomfortably, Priscilla usually managed to avoid the man.

She busied herself folding hose and watched from the corner of her eye as the tall, broad-shouldered investigator talked to Murph, then glanced her way—giving her a long, lingering look that she pretended not to see.

She hoped no one else noticed. The guys didn't need anything else to torment her with.

Roark examined the pile of charred paint cans and blackened rags, then he took a few pictures with a digital camera. Since everyone was watching him, Priscilla gave up trying to pretend she wasn't interested. She ambled closer so she could hear, too.

"Definitely arson, but not our boy," Roark said to Murph. *Our boy* was Roark's designation for the serial arsonist. "Probably a kid looking for a thrill. If it was the property owner wanting to collect insurance, he'd have gone to a little more trouble to hide his tracks."

The sound of Roark's Boston accent, still strong despite the years he'd spent in Texas, brought back unwanted memories. And his conclusions about this fire frustrated her. Not that she *wanted* the serial arsonist to set more blazes. On the other hand, with each fire he set, the potential existed for more clues to his identity—though so far he'd been damn clever about not leaving fingerprints or witnesses.

The collective mood relaxed as everyone continued about their business, putting away tools and ladders, joking and laughing now that the tension had eased. Priscilla continued to poke things with her pike pole.

"Hey, Pris, you going to the retirement party next week?" Ethan asked her. The captain in charge of the B shift at Station 59 was hanging up his hat.

"I can't. I have to attend…you know, a family event. My cousin's wedding is coming up, and she's having this froufrou dinner for all the bridesmaids at the Mansion."

Priscilla poked at a stump. Sparks flew out of it. "Someone douse this thing."

"Ooo, the Mansion." Otis strolled over with the booster line and sprayed down the stump. "I always wanted to go there. Need a date?"

Priscilla laughed. "Ruby wouldn't like that." Ruby was Otis's girlfriend and about to become wife number three. "Besides, my mother has a list of eligible candidates, should I want a date to this shindig. Which I don't."

"Uh-oh," Ethan said. "Sounds like your mother is still trying to fix you up."

Priscilla cringed inwardly. It must seem to everyone else that she couldn't get her own dates. The fact was, Priscilla didn't want to hook up with anybody. Her job kept her plenty busy. When she wasn't at the station, she was training for her paramedic certification. But her mother was concerned about her, worried that her only child was lonely after a nasty breakup last year.

Most of the time Priscilla refused her mother's matchmaking attempts. But occasionally she gave in—just to keep the peace. Since all the other bridesmaids would have husbands or boyfriends in attendance at the dinner, Priscilla would probably end up agreeing to a fix-up this time.

"Why don't you tell your mother to knock it off?" Ethan asked.

The question made perfect sense. Priscilla was not exactly shy and retiring when it came to telling people what to do. She knew she had a reputation as the C shift control freak, always trying to organize things to her satisfaction.

But telling her *mother* what to do was a whole different plate of deviled eggs. Lorraine Garner was an unstoppable force.

"I don't want to hurt her feelings," Priscilla said. "She tries so hard and she only wants me to be happy. I try to tell her I don't want a boyfriend…." And at this point she slid a look toward Roark, who had stopped talking with Murph and was blatantly eavesdropping. Damn. "But she assumes I'm pining away because I'm not attached. Going out on an occasional fix-up is easier than arguing."

And she didn't want to argue with her mother. She'd been a rebellious teenager, angry at the world, and she'd hurt her parents more than she'd realized with her obstinate determination to do things her way and have her misplaced revenge. Now that she was older and supposedly wiser, she tried to be more careful about balancing her wants and needs with their sensibilities. They were, after all, the only family she was likely to have, given her dismal track record with the opposite sex.

Ethan got a roll of yellow caution tape and tied one end to a fence post. "Would your mother lay off if you had a boyfriend?"

"Sure. I mean, I think so." When Priscilla had been dating Cory Levine the previous year and it appeared to be serious, her mother had been so happy. "But I don't have a boyfriend and I don't want one. Who has time, anyway? I don't see how you newlyweds do it." Ethan and Tony had both tied the knot during the past few months.

"How about a pretend boyfriend then?" Ethan suggested. "Tell your mom you're seeing someone."

"I've thought of that. But a fictional boyfriend won't cut it. She'd have to meet him, approve of him and hear wedding bells before she'd stop matchmaking."

Otis squirted the back of Priscilla's coat with his booster line, just to be ornery. "Why don't you take me home to meet your mama? Give her a heart attack and be done with it!" He cackled at his own humor, and Priscilla had to admit it was a little bit funny, thinking of how her parents would react if she brought home a forty-five-year-old, twice-married firefighter.

But then she sobered. Her mother's matchmaking efforts had become a problem. She couldn't attend any gathering without Lorraine thrusting some earnest young man at her. Some of them were very handsome and very nice. But Priscilla simply wasn't interested in putting herself out there again right now, going through the dating rituals. The angst and uncertainty drove her nuts.

Her gaze again slid covertly to Roark. They hadn't exactly dated; they'd slept together. Their affair had been all about stress relief, a strictly physical thing. That's what she'd told herself, anyway.

Roark had wanted to prolong their liaison. But the intensity of their times together had frightened Priscilla. She hadn't been able to control herself and she didn't like that feeling. So she'd put a stop to the relationship before it had really gotten started—before they'd had a chance to get to know each other, to open up and share who they really were. She hadn't been ready for that.

She might never be ready. She liked her life pretty well right now, living alone, answering to no one.

"Here's an idea," Ethan said. "Why don't you produce a real boyfriend?"

"I can't just materialize a boyfriend out of thin air," Priscilla said sensibly.

"What I mean is, get someone to pose as your boyfriend. Someone impeccable. Someone your mom couldn't possibly object to. Trot him out to meet your parents, hint around that it's serious. Do that, and your mother will be satisfied."

Priscilla had to admit the idea was attractive. The ploy might give her a few months of peace, anyway. "And where do you suggest I find this paragon of a fake boyfriend?" Although she didn't want to say so out loud, she didn't think her mother would approve of Priscilla dating a fellow firefighter. Lorraine had enough trouble with her daughter living one-third of her life in a firehouse with a bunch of men. But dating one of them?

"I have the perfect candidate," Ethan said, his eyes full of mischief, and Priscilla felt a stab of apprehension. Who did he have in mind? What had she stepped into? "Maybe," Ethan said, "your parents would approve of an arson investigator."

Priscilla gulped and glanced at Roark, startled to discover that he was almost right behind her, leaning against the fence. Silently she begged Roark to put in a quick refusal. But he didn't. He looked a little surprised at being put forward as a candidate to be Priscilla's fake boyfriend. But not unhappy.

"Hey, that's perfect," Otis said innocently, having no earthly idea that Priscilla and Roark shared a bit of their past. "Who could object to Roark? He's gainfully employed, he cleans up nice and he talks like some aristocrat. Epperson, what do you say? You want to make Priscilla's mom a happy woman?"

Priscilla would have liked to sink into the dirt. The last thing she wanted was Roark to play any type of boyfriend, fictional or otherwise. She was still several feet from him, but she couldn't stop her heart from racing. Her lips tingled, she was getting warm in places not mentioned in polite society and her hands itched to touch him, to muss up that perfectly groomed hair.

Priscilla looked to Roark, again praying he would say no, quickly and forcefully. But instead he wore a pensive expression, as if thinking over the proposition.

Then abruptly he smiled and looked straight at her, reminding her of a shark coming in for the kill. "I'm always willing to go the extra mile for a comrade. Sure, I'll help you out, Priscilla. I could be convincing, too. Very convincing."

A charged silence followed his statement. Jeez, did everyone in her unit now know that Priscilla and Roark had slept together?

Ethan broke the silence. "Then it's settled. Priscilla, your problems are over. All we needed was to put our heads together. You can thank me later."

Thank him? She was going to pinch his head off once they were some place without witnesses.

"Captain Epperson, don't listen to any of them," she said, pretending it was all a joke. "You're very kind to want to help, but I can handle my mother. Been doing it for a few years now."

Roark Epperson thought fast as Priscilla started to walk away. He needed a way to prolong the contact. He had questions and he wanted answers. "Priscilla?"

She turned. "Yes?"

"When you were in training, you seemed to take a special interest in arson investigation." And in the arson investigator, but that was a separate issue. "I could use some help collecting samples. I'm sure Lieutenant McCrae won't mind if I borrow you a few minutes."

Roark could see the turmoil in her eyes. She didn't want to be alone with him. Was she embarrassed that she'd shown him so much passion? Was she guilty about it? Was there another man in the picture?

They had shared very little personal information during their brief liaison. He knew she'd broken up with someone not long before they met, but she'd given him no details.

"Sure, I'll give you a hand," Priscilla said, deceptively casual.

He took her over to his car and handed her several clean empty cans and some plastic bags, then instructed her on what to collect from among the charred remains of the shed and how to package the evidence. She put on latex gloves and followed his instructions while he watched.

He'd been intrigued from the moment he'd laid eyes on her, the only woman in the class. At first he'd thought he had her pegged: too slender, too weak, too pampered. But in this case, first impressions had been totally wrong. She was astonishingly strong for a woman her size. And he had never seen anyone work harder to get through training. He'd spotted her on the obstacle course several times after hours, often by herself, practicing until she got it right.

Priscilla poked at some dead leaves near the chain-link fence, searching for evidence. "Hey, Captain, look at this."

She'd found a book of matches. "Good job. Could be very useful."

Carefully she used tweezers to collect the evidence and place it in a plastic bag. Roark, meanwhile, studied her face, imprinting it in his memory so he could think about it later—the slope of her cheek, the curve of her lower lip.

The physical chemistry between them had been undeniable from that first day. But it was her grit and determination—and her quick mind—that had truly fascinated him.

It might have come to nothing if she hadn't gotten stranded in the fire academy parking lot one rainy day with two flat tires. Someone—one of the male trainees who resented her outshining him, no doubt—had stuck a knife in her treads. Roark despised bullies, and though Priscilla had been perfectly willing to call her auto club, Roark had convinced her to let him take her tires to be repaired. Then he'd helped her put them back on.

Afterward they'd gone for coffee. And somehow they'd ended up in bed at his place.

They hadn't even made it out of bed before she'd called it a mistake, reminding him that it was ethically questionable at best for her to sleep with an instructor. Though he'd agreed with her in theory, he hadn't wanted to let her go. He'd never met such a fascinating mix of characteristics in a woman—tough, no-nonsense one minute, then giving him glimpses of finishing-school manners the next. A soft, musical voice and innocent blue eyes that didn't flinch at the sometimes raw language and tasteless jokes that were part of the firefighter culture.

She'd tried to resist him. She'd turned him down when he'd asked her out, claiming she was uncomfortable. She'd also mentioned that she'd had a recent breakup and wasn't ready to start seeing anyone else.

But then she'd shown up at his loft. Twice more. Each time, she'd chastised herself afterward, saying it was wrong for her to use him. She'd said she didn't know what had gotten into her, that she didn't normally behave so erratically.

After that last time, he knew she wouldn't be back and he had let her go—but only temporarily. If it was a bad breakup that plagued her, perhaps time would cure the problem. And so he'd left her alone, but he'd kept tabs on her. Eric Campeon, her captain, was a friend of his.

He'd always intended to follow up with Priscilla once she'd settled into life as a firefighter and had more time to recover from whatever jerk she'd previously been hooked up with. When he saw something he wanted, he went after it. He'd let his ex-wife, Libby, get away far too easily. Maybe they hadn't been right for each other in the long run, but he would never know—because he'd given up without a fight. Once he'd realized she didn't want to start a family, he'd been so stunned he'd just let her walk out.

He'd learned a lot in the ten years since then. The man he'd become never gave up without a fight. He had a reputation for pursuing every avenue when it came to catching an arsonist and he intended to be every bit as determined in his personal life.

Maybe Priscilla wasn't right for him, either. But he wouldn't know unless he spent more time with her. He wanted to know what was behind that tough-girl exterior.

He couldn't remember the last time a woman had made him feel the way Priscilla Garner did.

He forced his mind back to the investigation at hand. "You were the first to arrive at the fire?" Roark asked.

"Otis and I were."

"See anything unusual? Smell anything?"

"I'm not good at smells and I had my SCBA on. But the fire did seem unusually intense and hot."

"Not surprising, since the shed was full of lawn equipment and maintenance stuff. Gasoline, paint, turpentine. We're damn lucky the whole place didn't explode."

"The building was fully involved by the time we got to it. Probably whatever was going to explode had already done so. There were a lot of bystanders, but most of them had gone by the time you arrived."

"Any kids? Gang colors?"

Priscilla paused, searching her memory. "Two Hispanic

boys, maybe fifteen or sixteen. Probably should have been in school. One was wearing green and black—that's Dawg colors, right?"

"You got it."

She described them in detail, down to the fact one of them had a chipped tooth, the other a broken shoelace. "They seemed real curious."

"Could you recognize them?"

"I think so."

"Good. I might show you some mug shots." He already had an idea who those characters might have been. He'd talked to them before about some Dumpster fires, but he hadn't been able to prove anything. Maybe they'd escalated to sheds.

"So did I do something wrong?" he asked suddenly.

Priscilla straightened to look at him, and for the first time he sensed true regret from her. "No, you did nothing wrong. I was the one misbehaving." She smiled sadly.

"So why is it you run from me like I have typhoid?"

She returned to her task, meticulously labeling one of the evidence bags. "I told you before—I'd just come out of a relationship."

Okay, now he was getting somewhere. "So I was your rebound lover."

"Yes. And that really wasn't fair. You seemed like you wanted something more than a playmate, and I wasn't ready for anything like that."

"But that was months ago. Surely you've recovered from whatever your previous scumbag boyfriend did."

That got another smile out of her, not quite as sad this time. "What about that rag? Should I collect that?"

"Yes, and you're changing the subject."

"I just don't want a boyfriend," she blurted out, sounding a little desperate.

"I don't buy that. Nobody wants to spend all their nights alone."

She sighed and looked anywhere but at him. "It's complicated."

"I've got time."

"I don't understand it myself, so how could I explain it to you? But, trust me, you really wouldn't want me for a girlfriend. I have issues."

"Everyone has issues. You deal with them or you live with them, but you don't just stop living."

She straightened up and turned to face him, her gaze direct and unwavering. "The fact is, Roark, I like you too much. I was so anxious about the whole thing I just…needed to get away from it. I'm one of those people who can't stand uncertainty. I like to be in control. Around you, I had no control, and I really couldn't tolerate it."

Roark knew female logic was different than male logic, but this blew him away. "Let me get this straight—you liked me too much so you broke things off."

"I know that sounds crazy."

To put it mildly. "So you don't even want to try?"

"Even if I wanted to, I don't have time. Between work and paramedic training, I'm overscheduled as it is."

"And yet you still have time to go on these dates your mother sets up."

"Only once in a blue moon. Don't try to defeat this with logic, Roark. I'm surprised and flattered you would want anything to do with me after the way I behaved during training. But I'm not ready to date anyone except on the most casual basis. And you and I couldn't do it casual."

She was right about that. With Priscilla, he would not be content with seeing her once or twice a month.

He took the samples she'd collected. "McCrae is looking a little impatient with us. Guess I better let you go."

"Yeah. Thanks for letting me help with the evidence."

"You're a quick learner."

She turned to leave, but he couldn't resist a parting shot. "I could still be your fictional boyfriend." Not that the role would be a big stretch.

"Thanks, but no. I just need to be more firm with my mother."

Roark had done all he could do. He gave Priscilla one last long, steamy look, reminding her of what she was giving up. Then he walked away from her. Damn, it was hard knowing he'd never hear from her again.

Chapter Two

Twenty-four hours later, Priscilla wanted to eat her words.
She was helping her mother fix Sunday dinner and she
needed a boyfriend in the worst way.

Lorraine Garner, who was well known for her cooking
skills, had been only too happy when Priscilla had shown
an interest in the kitchen for the first time in her life. Now
that Priscilla had discovered how essential cooking was to
her popularity at the firehouse, she had practically begged
her mother to teach her to cook.

In between instructions on preparing lasagna, Lorraine
couldn't resist interrogating Priscilla.

"How is your nurse training going?" she asked as she
demonstrated how to properly crush garlic without even
chipping her manicure. She wore a cream-colored silk
dress and pearls around her neck and she never got a spot
on herself.

"It's paramedic training," Priscilla gently corrected,
"and it's going fine so far."

Her mother would probably be much happier if Priscilla
had become a nurse. She'd been horrified when her
daughter had announced she was going to leave the home

decor shop she'd been managing since she graduated from college and become a firefighter. Lorraine hadn't liked the whole blue-collar aspect of it, but even more than that she'd been worried for her daughter's safety.

Priscilla, however, had been bored to death as a shop-keeper. She'd wanted to do something active, something that would make a difference in the world. She'd needed to turn her life in an entirely new direction so she wouldn't brood about Cory.

She'd always been fascinated with fire trucks. She'd even played fireman when she was a little kid, rescuing her cousin Marisa's dolls over and over from various flaming tragedies. It was pure impulse that had prompted her to apply to the fire department, and she'd wondered at the time if she'd gone a little crazy. But the very first time she'd fought a blaze in training, she'd liked that feeling and wanted more of it.

Eventually Lorraine had come to accept her daughter's new vocation and had stopped hoping it was a phase she was going through. But she had not stopped trying to fix what she perceived to be Priscilla's tragic lack of social life.

"Are they going to give you time off to attend the bridesmaids' dinner?" her mother asked.

"Yes, I have that day off." And she knew what was coming next.

"Have you decided who you'll take as your escort?"

"Mother, I really don't think Marisa is going to care whether I bring a date to the dinner." Her cousin Marisa was the bride. Lorraine and Priscilla's aunt Clara, her mother's sister, had been pitting the girls against each other since they were babies.

"I just don't want people to feel sorry for you," Lorraine

said. "You know Aunt Clara thinks you somehow messed up your only chance to snag a husband."

"The breakup was hardly my fault." Cory, who had never shown the slightest fondness for children that Priscilla had seen, had nonetheless been devastated when Priscilla confessed that she would never be able to bear his children. When she'd brought up the possibility of adoption, he'd closed his mind. His heart had been set on biological children. And that had meant he most definitely would not be proposing marriage.

Priscilla had been shocked and then saddened by his attitude. She'd been sure Cory was "the one." But she hadn't known him as well as she'd imagined she did.

"Of course it wasn't your fault," Lorraine said. "But Clara doesn't know that. She doesn't know what really happened."

"And she's not going to either." It had taken Priscilla years to come to terms with the fact that she could never become pregnant, never carry her own child. She was sixteen when she'd gone in for surgery to have one of her ovaries removed. Just one. But the surgeon, after inspecting them, had declared they both needed to come out, and Priscilla's parents had signed the consent form on the spot.

She'd awakened from the surgery to the devastating news that she was now infertile, that she would have to take hormones for the next thirty or so years. And she had been angry that her parents had stolen her future from her.

Unreasonably angry, she realized some years later. Her parents had made the best decision they could at the time.

Priscilla had spent the past couple of years repairing her relationship with her parents and she hated to rock the boat now. But she did need to put a stop to her mother's matchmaking.

"Would it be so very difficult for you to bring a date to the bridesmaid's dinner?" Lorraine tried again.

"All right, Mother, who is he?"

Lorraine almost managed to hide her smile of triumph. "Remember the Conleys who lived next door to us?"

"Yeah. They moved to Miami or someplace, didn't they?"

"Yes. But young Bill has moved back recently. And he wants to get into the social scene here."

Priscilla gasped as memories resurfaced. At age twelve, "young Bill" had worn a white belt and a pocket protector, and the rubberbands on his braces were always shooting out of his mouth.

She shook her head. "No. No can do."

"Priscilla, he's so handsome now! You would not recognize him. And he's an orthodontist. Anyway, it's just one date." The pleading note in Lorraine's voice nearly did Priscilla in. Her mother had such a way of manipulating her, and it drove Priscilla wild even as she fell victim to it.

"I can't, Mother, really. I'm…well, I'm seeing someone." Even as she said it, she knew she was heading for disaster.

"Really?" Lorraine's nose twitched. "Who is he? How come you didn't say something earlier?"

"It was so new and so fragile, and I didn't know if it was going to work. I didn't want to get your hopes up."

"But it's working out?" Lorraine asked, her eyes filled with hope. "Who is he? Please end the suspense."

Priscilla knew her mother was hoping the mystery boyfriend wasn't a firefighter. "He's… He's an arson investigator." The words just popped out of her mouth.

Lorraine smiled. "How interesting. Tell me more."

"His name is Roark Epperson." After that, it became easy to tell her the rest. He was in his midthirties, extremely handsome and came from a wealthy family in Massachusetts.

"Win, did you hear that?" Lorraine asked of Priscilla's father, who had wandered into the kitchen to get a refill on his wine. "Priscilla's dating an arson investigator."

"I heard," Priscilla's father said, sounding cautious. "I think I've seen that guy on TV." Generally Winfield Garner was content to remain at a distance from Priscilla's social life, letting his wife do all the organizing. But not today, apparently. "Does he talk like a Kennedy?"

Priscilla couldn't help smiling. That did seem to be the feature that everyone remembered about Roark. Well, women first remembered that he was mouthwateringly gorgeous and then they remembered the accent. "He's the one. They interviewed him the other night about the serial arsonist."

"An arson investigator," Lorraine said, trying it on for size. "That's really kind of interesting, isn't it, Win?"

The timer went off, indicating the lasagna noodles were ready. "So you can bring this Roark to the bridesmaids' dinner, right?" Lorraine said as she strained the noodles.

"He wouldn't know anyone."

"Why don't you ask him? And if he can't come to the dinner, what about the wedding itself?"

Eek. Roark would see her in that hideous pink monstrosity of a bridesmaid's dress. It might almost be worth it, though, to watch how Roark would weather the combined scrutiny of her entire extended family. By offering to play the role of her devoted boyfriend, he had no idea what he would be getting himself into.

"We'll see."

He was five minutes late.

Priscilla sat at a bistro table at the Nodding Dog, a cute little coffee shop in Oak Cliff's trendy Bishop Arts district, waiting for Roark.

If things worked out as she hoped, Roark would attend one function with her and her parents would be relieved, if only temporarily, that she wouldn't spend the rest of her life alone. Snobby Aunt Clara would be suitably impressed. And Priscilla wouldn't have to produce a flesh-and-blood boyfriend again for months.

She checked her watch again and took a sip of her latte. Then she saw him.

He looked as if he'd just stepped out of the pages of *GQ*, in perfectly creased khaki pants and a pale yellow shirt, the sleeves rolled up to the elbow in a sort of casually rumpled but still stylish way. For a few seconds she drank in the sight of him. Then he looked her way and she schooled her face.

She would just die if he knew he could melt her on the spot simply by looking at her. Actual skin-to-skin contact might cause her to spontaneously combust.

He walked up to the counter and ordered, and the pretty barista batted her eyelashes and blushed as she poured his coffee. He paid, chatting and smiling easily. Did he even know the effect he had on women?

He joined Priscilla at her small table, and she wished she'd chosen a larger one. He was so close she could see the tiny shaving nick on his jaw and smell his aftershave. It made her think of being on a mountaintop.

With her clothes off.

"I see you found the place." Why did she sound so inane? She'd had no problem talking to him that first night, when he'd helped her with her flat tires. She'd opened up to him, confessing how alone she felt sometimes, isolated from the other trainees. Tony and Ethan had befriended her, but back then she'd still felt a bit of an outsider even with them, since the two men already had been best friends for fifteen years.

Roark had been a sympathetic ear. He'd offered her encouragement that she'd needed to hear. A strong shoulder to lay her head on.

She'd been in a vulnerable state at that point in her life, she reminded herself—she'd still been smarting from Cory's cold rejection. But she was stronger now.

Roark took an appreciative sip from his mug. "I've been here before. Best coffee in Oak Cliff." He drank plain black coffee. No mochaccino whip for Roark.

She tucked that fact into a corner of her mind. Sometimes, when she couldn't sleep, she remembered the little intimacies she had shared with Cory. He knew she loved the scent of freshly washed sheets; she knew he couldn't stand green bell peppers. Would she ever be that close to a man again? Did she want to be?

She had a hard time imagining it. Sex was one thing. But the secret looks, the private jokes, the cozy breakfasts… How had she shared all those things with Cory, and yet missed some of the most fundamental aspects of his personality?

Like the fact that not being able to have his own biological children with his wife was a deal breaker?

She swallowed the last few sips of her latte.

"Let's take a walk," Roark suggested, gulping down the remainder of his coffee. "The weather is gorgeous."

She didn't want to walk in the gorgeous weather with Roark. She wanted to conclude their business and get away from him, because already she was feeling that familiar lethargy steal over her, that urge to open up, to trust him.

"So," he said as they exited the coffee shop, "I'm guessing you really, really need a fake boyfriend to get your mother off your back." He raised a single eyebrow at her. "Unless you've decided I'm not such a bad guy after all and maybe you want to get to know me better."

She quickened her step, striding down the sidewalk on Seventh Street. She did want to know him better. On the surface there was nothing wrong with him. He was smart and dedicated to his work and he'd helped her out of a jam when she'd had those two flat tires. But Cory had looked pretty good on the surface—and deeper, too.

How could she tell if Roark was all that he appeared to be?

"I need a fake boyfriend," she said.

He matched her stride, managing to do so without seeming to hurry. "What do you want me to do?"

"It's just one date. To my cousin's bridesmaids' dinner. It's at the Mansion." As if the bribe of a fancy dinner would hold sway with him. "It's next Friday. I realize it's short notice, but…"

He swore softly. "I can't make it then. I'm speaking at a conference out of town. Sorry, Priscilla."

"Oh." She didn't know whether to feel relieved or disappointed. "You could come to the wedding, but that's probably more of an ordeal than you bargained for." She paused to look in the window of an antiques shop.

They had slowed, Priscilla noticed. Now they were just strolling along like any couple. An older woman passed them and smiled insipidly, and Priscilla wondered what she was thinking. Young couple in love?

"Are you close to your cousin?" Roark asked.

"We used to be like sisters."

"Used to be?"

"She kind of dumped me in high school, when I had some sticky problems she didn't want to deal with."

"How rude. What kind of problems?"

"Oh, you know, teenage rebellion." Which involved a stint of hanging out with a bad crowd just for the shock value. She couldn't really blame Marisa for keeping her distance.

Roark clearly wasn't satisfied with her dismissive answer, but he didn't push.

How did Roark do this, anyway? Ten minutes in his presence, and she was blurting out embarrassing personal things.

"So when is the wedding?" he asked. "I don't mind weddings."

"November second." She half hoped he'd be busy then, too. But he checked his BlackBerry and confirmed he was free.

"I have to be at the church two hours early, so you can meet me there."

"Nonsense. What kind of a lousy boyfriend would I be if I didn't pick you up? We want your mother to think I'm a gentleman, right?"

"All right, but you're going to be bored."

"I doubt that."

The blatant interest in his gaze alarmed her. "Roark, this is pretend, right? I mean, you're not doing this because you want to continue…go back to…I mean—" She stared hard through the window of an art gallery at an ugly ceramic bowl.

"Yes, I want to do those things. Continue where we left off, go back to when we were involved."

"But that's not why I asked you to help."

"I know that. I'm planning to change your mind."

"No. You can't do that."

"I can't?" He gave her a challenging look, his hand still on her arm.

She pulled away. "No, you can't. Roark, you have to promise me you won't try to, you know…"

"Win you over?" His sexy mouth cocked into a half smile. "Seduce me."

Roark had the nerve to laugh. "You can't tell me you're *that* vulnerable to my wicked ways."

"Actually, yes, damn it, I am. You're impossible to resist. I can't imagine how you've managed to stay single, but I can only guess it's because you're a player, and that is the last type of person I need in my life."

To her surprise, Roark looked contrite. "All right. I'll try to behave myself."

"You can't touch me."

"Aren't you trying to convince people we're an item?"

"All I need is a warm, suitably male body at my side. If you give me besotted looks every now and then, so much the better, but no further acting is required."

"You mean like this?" And he did a pretty good imitation of a basset hound yearning for a bone.

Somehow he made her laugh, and her anxiety receded. "Maybe not quite that besotted." They worked out a few more details, and the deal was struck. Roark would provide the services of one fake boyfriend. But Priscilla couldn't help wondering what she would end up giving in return.

IT WAS LUNCHTIME ON the C shift at Fire Station 59, and Priscilla was in charge. She had practiced the vegetable lasagna at home and it had come out tasting really good. So she'd asked Captain Campeon to give her another chance in the kitchen.

She wasn't sure why it was so important to her, except that her previous gastronomical disasters were just one more thing that set her apart from the guys—all of whom seemed to know their way around a kitchen. Even Ethan and Tony, who hadn't started out particularly gifted, had caught on.

As the guys ambled in to the large eat-in kitchen, grumbling about the possible culinary torture Priscilla would subject them to, she pulled a large casserole dish out of the oven and set it down on the long table.

"Be afraid. Be very afraid." The comment came from Otis.

"What is that stuff?" Tony asked suspiciously. "It looks weird." Ethan elbowed him, and Tony quickly added, "But it smells good and I'm sure it's delicious."

She gave him a smile for his loyalty. Tony and Ethan had often been the only ones to take her side during training and those first few weeks here at Station 59, when she was subject to attack from guys who objected to women firefighters in general and her in particular.

"It's vegetable lasagna," Priscilla announced with a flourish.

For her trouble, she got groans all around.

"God save us from women trying to make us eat healthy," said Bing Tate, who was one of the most annoying men Priscilla had ever known. Though most of the other guys grudgingly had come to accept the rookies, Bing continued to make caustic comments at every opportunity—especially if the captain wasn't within earshot. And he wasn't at the moment.

"Where's the captain?" Priscilla asked as she cut the lasagna into large squares so it would cool faster.

"He's got someone in his office."

Priscilla hoped whoever it was wouldn't keep the captain so long that he missed a hot lunch. She liked Captain Campeon. He was stern and humorless, but he kept strict order, and she approved of that. She didn't function well in a chaotic environment.

Priscilla noticed no one was touching the salad she'd put out. "You can eat the salad while the lasagna cools."

She served some salad for herself. The mixture of field greens topped with fresh garden tomatoes tasted pretty good as far as she was concerned. But her fellow firefighters seemed to thrive on red meat and a variety of breaded, fried foods—along with a steady diet of action movies on TV, twangy country music on the radio and off-color jokes just about everywhere.

She was adjusting.

The guys went for the whole-wheat rolls and butter she'd put out. Only Bing tried a little bit of the salad, making faces as he chewed.

"Hey, Priscilla," Bing said. "Where'd you get these leafy things? Did you pick 'em from that weedy patch out back?"

She just shook her head. The only lettuce most of these guys had ever seen was the soggy iceberg they put on their hamburgers. She started to say something to that effect, but the captain chose that moment to appear with his guest in tow.

Roark.

Priscilla's heart thundered so loud she was sure everyone would hear it. Tony and Ethan knew of the deal she'd struck with Roark, but no one else did. She hoped *he* wouldn't say anything. If he did, there would be no end to the teasing she would get, and any credibility she'd built up would disintegrate.

The others greeted Roark like an old friend—which he was by now. Since the men who'd died in the warehouse fire had come from this company, Roark's investigation had brought him to their station quite a few times.

"Captain Epperson is gonna have some lunch with us," Campeon said. "Then he wants to talk to you—all of you, one on one."

The solemn note in the captain's voice was troubling. Everyone was wondering what this was about. Since this station responded first to the warehouse fire, Roark had no doubt interviewed everyone already, probably more than once. Why do it again?

But Roark reassured them with his easy smile. "You guys don't mind if I mooch some lunch, do you?" He didn't make eye contact with Priscilla, which was a relief. Perhaps he didn't want to be ribbed any more than she did.

"Join us at your own risk," Bing said. "Priscilla made lunch." He nodded toward the lasagna pan. "We think it might still be moving." A couple of the other guys couldn't help laughing. Even Tony cracked a smile.

She couldn't really blame them. Her previous meals had been pretty awful. But she was sure this would be different. Yes, it was a vegetarian dish, but her father loved it. Even Cory had loved it when Lorraine had served it at a Garner family dinner, and he was a meat-and-potatoes guy all the way.

Still, she didn't like Roark witnessing the guys making fun of her. She didn't like appearing incompetent in front of him—or anyone.

Priscilla quickly served the squares of lasagna, oozing

with cheese and fragrant with fresh herbs. The men stared at their plates, but no one seemed willing to take that first bite.

Finally Roark took a leap of faith. "This looks good." He put a big forkful in his mouth. Others followed suit.

Priscilla took a bite, too—and almost spit it out. Her mouth was on fire. It tasted as if the sauce contained a quart of jalapeño pepper sauce, though she'd used only a drop or two.

Horrified, Priscilla looked around the table to see faces turning red, eyes watering, hands grabbing for glasses of tea or milk to try to wash down the offending substance.

"Um, interesting," Tony said, barely managing to swallow. "Where did you get the recipe, Pris? The Cataclysmic Heartburn Cookbook?"

"It's my mother's recipe," she said, bewildered. She'd followed the recipe exactly. There was no way….

Then she saw that one man at the table hadn't taken a bite. Bing Tate was trying to hide his mirth—and not doing a good job of it.

Suspecting she'd been sabotaged, she got up and stalked over to the cabinet were they kept spices and found the bottle of jalapeño sauce she'd bought recently. It was nearly empty.

She marched back to the table. "Bing Tate, did you dump a whole bottle of jalapeño sauce in my sauce when I wasn't looking?" She remembered he'd been in the kitchen that morning, getting a refill on his coffee and taking a little too long to do it.

"Who, me?" he said with feigned innocence. Obviously she'd found her culprit. Though what Bing had done was mean, she was relieved the disaster wasn't her fault this time.

She struggled not to react with anger. Practical jokes were a part of life around here, a natural product of boredom and too much testosterone, and anyone who wasn't a good sport only got hit with more foolish mayhem.

But no one else seemed to think Bing's joke was funny. Otis put some more salad on his plate and drowned it with ranch dressing. "The salad's good, anyway, Pris," he said grudgingly, and she could have kissed his shiny bald head.

"Anyone want a ham sandwich?" Priscilla asked brightly. "I can't mess that up."

"The guys can make their own sandwiches," Campeon said, clearly irritated by the incident. "I think Captain Epperson would like to get on with his interviews. Garner, he can start with you."

"Me?" The order took her by surprise. "I wasn't even at the warehouse fire." She'd still been in training, and up until now Roark hadn't ever included the rookies in his investigation.

"You," Roark confirmed. "We can talk in the captain's office."

Chapter Three

Roark's breath caught in his throat the way it did every time he saw Priscilla. Even in the loose-fitting department uniform of dark pants and a golf shirt, her caramel-brown hair pulled back in a braid, she looked touchable. He stepped around Eric Campeon's desk and sat in the captain's chair, putting a large amount of polished oak between them.

"Is that the kind of crap you have to put up with all the time?" He'd been surprised by the protective instincts that had arisen when he realized she'd been the victim of a mean joke. And then he'd been impressed by the cool, controlled way she'd handled the situation.

"It used to be worse." She took the chair opposite. "I wasn't very popular when I was first assigned here. None of us were, because we were taking over for the three men who died. And, let's face it, it's pretty hard to fill the shoes of a martyr."

"I can imagine."

"But we all just kept our mouths shut and did our jobs, and gradually the others began to accept us. Except maybe for Bing Tate."

"The guy's an ass." Roark had seen how hard Priscilla was trying, how much she was hoping the guys would like her lasagna. When he'd realized what Tate had done, he'd wanted to wring the scrawny jerk's neck.

Priscilla shrugged. "I'll get him back in some passive-aggressive way. Maybe I'll short-sheet his bed."

Roark didn't think she would. She wouldn't stoop to Bing's level. He liked that about her. She wasn't vengeful or petty. He'd seen her take a lot of crap during training, and she'd always been a good sport.

He suspected sometimes the taunting had hurt more than she let on. She wouldn't show any weakness, though. Not Priscilla.

"So what's going on?" she asked. "Why do you want to talk to me?"

Truthfully, he would have invented any excuse to get her alone for a few minutes. Unfortunately he did have a legitimate reason. "I think the serial arsonist is someone connected to the fire service."

Priscilla's eyes widened. "Oh, no. I really hope you're wrong."

It was a sad fact that many arsonists turned out to be firefighters or former firefighters. A person might be drawn to the fire service because he wanted to serve his community or save property or because the lifestyle appealed to him or his father and grandfather were firefighters. But it might just as easily be an unhealthy fascination with fire.

Clearly this particular perpetrator wasn't your average firebug—a teenage mischief maker or someone out to collect on insurance. This guy knew a lot about fires—and how not to get caught setting them.

"We don't know for sure, but the evidence is leaning that

way," Roark said. "The fires aren't set just to watch something burn. The guy is deliberately trying to injure or kill firefighters, which indicates he has some emotional connection. I've been investigating every firefighter who's left the department under less-than-favorable circumstances in the past ten years, but so far none of them look good as a suspect. I'm wondering now if it's someone still currently employed, maybe someone who got passed over for promotion."

"But surely no one from this shift. I mean, they were all here when the warehouse fire started. They couldn't have started it."

Roark lowered his voice. "This isn't common knowledge, but there was a timer on the ignition device. The whole thing could have been set up several hours before."

"I don't want to believe this. It can't be any of the guys here."

"What about Tate?"

"Not even him. Every one of those guys out there has grieved for the men who died. I've watched them."

"It's only a possibility at this point. It could be anybody, from any shift, any station."

"So why are you talking to me about this? How could I possibly help?"

"Maybe you weren't here for the warehouse fire, but you've been around for several months now. You could see or hear something as easily as anyone. For instance, if there's anyone with an ax to grind with the department— any scuttlebutt going around—that's the kind of information I need."

"You want me to rat on my brothers?"

"To stop this guy from killing more firefighters? Yeah.

And he will kill again. If he goes unchecked, it's only a matter of time." The arsonist often left a little surprise for the firefighters. Once, it was a vicious dog that had bitten Murph McCrae when he'd tried to rescue it. Another time, the serial arsonist had left a homemade bomb, though fortunately the thing hadn't detonated.

Priscilla sagged a little in her chair. "I know he's got to be stopped."

"Anything you tell me is confidential," Roark continued. "I'm asking everyone the same thing. If there's anyone I should look at more closely..."

"I wish I could help. But I'm the last person anyone would trust or confide in," she said a little testily.

"Just keep your eyes and ears open."

"I don't like this. I don't like it at all."

"Believe me, I don't like it either. And I hope I'm wrong. But it's my responsibility to catch this guy, and I'll do whatever it takes. Even if it ticks people off." He would not allow another person to die on his watch.

"Is that all?" She stood, preparing to make her escape.

He stood, too, and stepped around the desk. He didn't want to end their meeting on such a negative note. "Have you told your mother all about me?"

She nodded, inching away from him, putting more distance between them. "Mother is thrilled. She got on the Internet so she could read all the newspaper articles you've been quoted in. She printed them off to show my aunt Clara."

"Aunt Clara being...the mother of the bride?"

"Good guess. She and my mom are sisters and they're intensely competitive. It's killing Mother that Clara's daughter is getting married before hers, especially since..."

"Since what?"

"Well, since last year Mother thought she heard wedding bells. Turned out to be a funeral dirge."

"The guy you were rebounding from?"

She nodded. "When we broke up, Mother was more disappointed than I was, I think."

"And now she has something to pin her hopes on again."

Priscilla nodded, wincing. "I hadn't realized it was going to get this complicated. I thought this plan would buy me some peace, at least for a few months. Maybe I should claim we broke up at the last minute."

Roark smiled. "I wouldn't do that to your mother. But I do have one question for you."

"Yes?"

"How is anyone going to believe I'm your boyfriend when you look like a scared rabbit every time I get within two feet of you?"

"I'll do better," she promised hastily.

"Maybe we should rehearse. You know, practice looking fondly at each other. Hold hands." With every suggestion, her eyes got a little wider.

"That's not necessary," she said. "We'll do fine." Then she did escape. But Roark wasn't too discouraged—if anything, her skittishness raised the bar. Would he even want a woman if she was a pushover? He enjoyed the challenge.

ROARK HAD BEEN LOOKING forward to this day like a kid counting the days to Christmas. The wedding of two people he'd never met. He could devote the whole evening to Priscilla. She would be his captive, stuck at the wedding and unable to flee. And he intended to see how far that could take him.

He pulled up to the curb in front of her two-story frame house in Oak Cliff's historic district and cut the engine. He was late by five minutes, which was probably good. He didn't want to appear *too* eager. He checked his hair in the mirror and then laughed at himself for being vain. His brothers and sisters had always teased him about that, about the fact that he liked to dress well and look his best even if he was just running to the grocery store for milk.

When he rang the bell, Tony Veracruz promptly opened the front door. He held a crying baby in one arm and a cat in the other and he was wearing a big smile.

Roark had been to this house before. Tony had invited him over a couple of times to play shuffleboard. He knew that Priscilla owned the house and lived in the upper apartment, renting the main floor to Tony. But he'd never been up the stairs.

"Priscilla will be down in a minute," Tony said.

They were standing in a small vestibule. A set of steps to the immediate left of the door led upstairs. Roark wanted to see what kind of apartment a woman like Priscilla called home. But she apparently didn't want him up there.

"Come on in," Tony was saying. "Sorry about the racket. Josephina is teething."

Last he'd heard, Tony didn't have a baby. A nine-year-old daughter, yes. And there was Jasmine, perched on a chair in the living room, holding a baby bottle.

"Jasmine and I are babysitting," Tony explained. "The baby belongs to Julie's chef. Her regular sitter is sick." Julie was Tony's wife and also the owner of Brady's Tavern and Tearoom, across the street from Fire Station 59.

Roark could see that Tony and his daughter had been exerting considerable effort to distract the baby from her teething pain. Toys of every description were spread out over the coffee table and a large area rug in the living room.

"Jasmine," Tony said, "run upstairs and tell Pris her *boyfriend* is here."

Startled, Jasmine stared at Roark. "Priscilla has a boyfriend?" She sounded almost scandalized.

"Go," Tony said.

When she'd gone, Roark asked, "You aren't giving Priscilla trouble over this fake boyfriend thing, are you?"

"Are you kidding? After all the grief she gave me when Julie and I got engaged, I couldn't let a golden opportunity like this pass by." He paused, put the cat down and shifted the baby to his other shoulder. "I shouldn't do that, huh?"

"It's a bit of a sore spot with her, I think," Roark said carefully. "She'd probably never admit that."

"Yeah, heaven forbid she show any weakness." Tony jiggled the baby and offered her a teething ring, which she promptly rejected. "Aw, come on, little one."

"Here, let me try," Roark said.

"You? You don't have kids, do you?"

"Just an endless stream of nieces and nephews. But I spend as much time with them as I can. Whenever I go home to visit, someone is *always* teething." He took the baby, who wore a ruffled pink dress and matching booties, and held her up, looking her in the face. "Hi, Josephina. Can you look at me?" And he proceeded to make faces at her while Tony tried not to laugh.

The baby was so startled by the faces that she did stop crying, at least for the moment. Roark gently swung her back and forth. She stared wide-eyed at him.

"How'd you do that?" Tony asked.

"It's probably just the novelty of a new face," Roark admitted. "She might start crying again any minute."

"Let me try it," Tony said, holding out his hands. Before he could take the baby, though, Jasmine came running down the steps.

"Dad, wait till you see this. You won't believe it!"

Moments later, a cloud of florid pink chiffon barely contained in a clear plastic bag descended the stairs, and somewhere behind it was Priscilla—in curlers.

The men froze, and even Josephina, who'd been cooing softly, went silent. She seemed to be staring at the spectacle, too.

"I don't want to hear anything about cotton candy or Glinda the Good Witch or…or Martians," Priscilla said as she descended. Carefully—probably because she couldn't see her feet. "Not one word."

Tony whistled. "Do you have to get permission from Pepto-Bismol to wear that color?"

Roark bit his lip. He had to admit, the bridesmaid's gown was a ghastly hue.

He hadn't expected Priscilla to show up for their first—and possibly only—date in curlers, either. Pink plastic rollers like his mother used to wear. He didn't see why she had to resort to such extreme measures. Her natural hair, straight and thick and the most gorgeous dark honey color, didn't need any improvement.

Priscilla finally looked at Roark, and what she saw almost made her miss a step. Roark, holding a baby as if it were the most natural thing in the world. She felt an unexpected contraction in the vicinity of her womb. And the way Roark was looking at her, as if she were a mountain of strawberry ice cream and he was hot fudge, didn't help matters. She had thought the curlers would put him off.

She pulled herself together. "Hi, Roark. There's still time to change your mind."

Roark shook his head. "Not a chance. I want to see you actually wearing that dress. It's bigger than you."

"And it weighs more than my turnout gear."

"I think it makes you look like Cinderella," said Jasmine, who loved all things pink and girlie. She had begged Priscilla to model the dress when she'd brought it home a few days earlier.

Priscilla spared a smile for the girl. "Thank you, Jasmine. But, remember, it's not the dress that makes the princess."

"I know, it's the *inner* princess," Samantha said with a giggle.

Priscilla ruffled the girl's dark mop of hair, then grabbed a couple of bulging shopping bags sitting near the bottom of the stairs. She looked at Roark. "Are we taking Josephina with us?"

"Oh, um, no." He handed the baby to Tony, then focused his attention back on Priscilla. "You ready?" He had to raise his voice to be heard over Josephina's renewed screams.

"I know I don't *look* ready. But Marisa has a legion of makeup artists and hair torturers waiting for me at the church."

Priscilla was momentarily taken aback once again when she saw Roark's car—a red Porsche. "Quite a step up from the black Suburban."

"That's my work car. *This* is my play car."

Pretty nice toy, Priscilla thought as she stuffed her shopping bags, containing shoes and other accessories, in the tiny trunk. Where was she going to put the dress? The car didn't have a backseat to speak of. "We need a sidecar for the dress."

"I think all three of us will fit." He gallantly opened the passenger door, then held the dress while Priscilla got herself situated. He gently draped the dress over her, though he had to try three times before he was able to stuff the mountain of pink chiffon inside.

And then they were off, Roark deftly maneuvering his macho machine through the twilight of an early fall evening. The weather was magnificent, with just a touch of chill in the air. Priscilla wished she could enjoy it. But she was too tense. The next few hours were going to be tedious. Marisa and her mother would be walking, talking high-anxiety machines while eight bridesmaids—eight!— tried to do makeup and hair and change their clothes in that tiny bride's room.

Priscilla didn't like pandemonium, especially when she had no chance of controlling or organizing things. She would be at the mercy of her family. And Roark would get to see it all.

He would probably run for the hills.

"Okay," she said when the silence had stretched too long. "I've been thinking about this, and here's the story. In case someone asks how we met, how long we've been dating, that sort of thing."

"Okay."

"Let's keep it simple. We met a couple weeks ago, when you were called to a fire that I worked. You asked me some questions about the fire, then you asked me out to dinner the next night and we've been seeing each other ever since."

"Where did we go on our first date?" he asked. "Everyone always asks that."

"Um… We went out for pizza."

"I could do better than that. How about we went to Newport's?" Newport's was one of Dallas's best seafood restaurants.

"Too dressy for a first date. How about Havana Nights?" Havana Nights was a hot new Cuban restaurant in Bishop Arts.

"Done. Are we serious?"

"Our relationship, you mean? It has potential to be serious," she said carefully.

"Do we hear wedding bells?"

Priscilla's heart skipped a beat. "You don't have to take it that far. Do you know where you're going, by the way?"

"To that humongous church in Highland Park? The one that looks like a medieval cathedral, complete with gargoyles?"

"That's the one. You've been there?"

"Actually, I got married there."

"You've been married?" she blurted out. She wasn't sure why that surprised her. A man as good-looking as he was seldom reached his midthirties without at least one trip to the altar.

"Only for a couple of years, when I was younger."

"Were there children?" The image of Roark holding Josephina flashed through her mind.

"No."

She gathered by his clipped answer that she might have touched on a sensitive issue.

"Libby and I wanted different things. We married pretty young and we had some idealistic notions about what marriage would be all about. But we were still growing and changing and figuring out who we were. And in the end…our goals in life were polar opposites. Maybe if we'd gotten counseling or something…" He shrugged. "But we were just dumb kids."

"It's still sad." She processed this new information about Roark, trying to fit it to the man as she knew him. "You don't seem jaded, like a lot of divorced people are."

"*Cautious* would be more accurate. But not without hope." He smiled enigmatically at her. Instantly her chest tightened in a not-unpleasant way.

"I hope this won't bring back sad memories for you," she said.

He shrugged. "I got over all that a long time ago."

She wondered. Did anybody truly get completely over a divorce? She and Cory hadn't even gotten to the wedding-plan stage before their relationship had ended, but she wasn't sure she would ever be able to talk about it as casually as Roark talked about his previous marriage.

She shivered.

"You cold?" Roark asked.

"Maybe a little."

He inched the thermostat up a bit.

They took advantage of the valet parking that had been arranged—Priscilla didn't want to drag the dress any farther than she had to. Roark courteously carried the rest of her things, so she could hold the dress well off the ground.

The church *did* look like a medieval cathedral. Since she'd been attending services here her whole life, she'd never thought about it much. But it was grand to the point of ostentation. Everything was white and gray marble, punctuated by intricate stained glass and pseudoancient tapestries.

The wedding consultant, whose name was Elisha, greeted Priscilla like a long-lost best friend. "The others are all here. Hurry, now, hurry!" Then she gave Roark a quick once-over, gasped daintily and directed them toward the dressing room.

"You want me to go to the dressing room with you?" Roark asked, looking doubtful. "I can just go sit in the church."

"Oh, no," Priscilla said, "you *have* to come with me. My mother is already half-inclined to believe I made you up." She grabbed his hand and dragged him with her. A few seconds later she realized she had voluntarily touched him. As soon as he appeared to be following willingly, she dropped his hand like a hot coal.

She knocked on the dressing room door, which opened instantly. Her mother stood blocking the entry and looking worried. "Priscilla. Where have you been? I was starting to get concerned."

Priscilla checked her watch. She was only five minutes late. "Sorry, traffic was bad." Which was true. Traffic in Dallas was always bad.

"Hang your dress up over there, but don't get it mixed up with the others. Christina will do your makeup as soon as she gets done with Judith's. And then Rebecca will do your…" Her tirade halted abruptly when she saw Roark. "Oh. I'm sorry, I didn't realize you weren't alone. This must be your young man."

Gawd, where did her mother come up with these archaic expressions? She'd grown up in the sixties. Surely she hadn't referred to *her* boyfriends as "young men."

"Mother, this is Roark Epperson," Priscilla said dutifully. "Roark, my mother, Lorraine Garner."

Roark took her mother's hand and squeezed it. "Nice to meet you, Mrs. Garner."

Lorraine's attention was so fixed on Roark she forgot she was in the middle of giving Priscilla her instructions. Priscilla couldn't help but smile. Roark had that effect on women, no matter what their age.

She was sure Roark could hold his own, so she skulked past her mother and into the room where she could properly greet the bride with a dainty hug.

"You look beautiful, Marisa," Priscilla said, meaning it. Although her cousin was still in a dressing gown, her lush, curly black hair had been piled on top of her head in a style worthy of a Greek goddess. "You're just…radiant."

"Thank you," Marisa said regally. Then she whispered, "The guy is *gorgeous*. And you let him see you in curlers!"

"Couldn't be avoided. You know my hair doesn't hold a curl for more than five minutes."

"And mine frizzes in the humidity. Remember when we used to want to trade hair?"

Priscilla nodded and swallowed hard. She hadn't thought she would get mushy—especially because Marisa and she hadn't been as close in recent years. They'd gone to different colleges, cultivated different friends. But they'd shared a lot when they'd been younger, including their attempts to thwart their pushy mamas.

"Come and meet everyone, Roark," Lorraine was saying. And she performed introductions. To his credit, Roark didn't even flinch when seven women, some of them wearing identical hideous pink dresses, all tried to introduce themselves at once. Three of them were already married, yet to a woman they eyed Roark with predatory interest.

Even the prospective bride, who should have had thoughts only for her groom, sparkled a bit as Roark was introduced.

"Thank you so much for coming," Marisa simpered. "It's *such* a pleasure to have you at my wedding. I've seen you on TV."

"The pleasure's mine." His voice was low and sexy as he shot Priscilla a look that could melt cold steel.

Again Priscilla was sure everyone in the room read between the lines and knew they'd slept together. This was *not* what she'd asked him to do.

"Well," Roark said briskly, "I'll let you ladies get back to…whatever it is women do before a wedding." Every female in the room but Priscilla giggled—even her aunt Clara, who was normally about as giggly as a *Star Wars* storm trooper.

Priscilla walked him to the door. "You're supposed to be devoted and besotted," she whispered, "not hot to trot. Try to remember the difference!"

Roark tried not to grin at her fierce reprimand. He deserved it. But hiding his growing attraction to Priscilla was getting more difficult with each passing minute he spent with her.

Chapter Four

Roark found a place to sit near the back of the massive church. He hadn't been here since his own wedding; it had been his ex-wife's church, not his. Dallas was her home turf, and they'd ended up settling here so she could work for her father's company. Roark hadn't liked moving so far from his family, but he'd wanted Libby to be happy.

The church, though grandiose, wasn't an unpleasant place. It was quiet, with only occasional whispered conversation as early wedding guests greeted each other. He had plenty of time and space to dream—maybe too much.

He couldn't help thinking about Priscilla. He hadn't meant to send her that searing look and make a suggestive comment right in front of her mother. It had just come out that way.

He vowed he would try to be more reserved about his besottedness. But the way she looked, even in the ridiculous curlers, made it damned difficult. It was those big, soft eyes, so mysterious, so...vulnerable.

Gradually the church filled, and soon soft strains of organ music filled the air. The procession of flower girls and bridesmaids began, and Roark found himself biting his tongue to keep from laughing. They looked like a parade of giant pink marshmallows in fancy footwear.

When Priscilla finally appeared, second to last, his reaction was very different. Like the other bridesmaids, she wore a floral wreath in her hair. Her long golden-brown hair wasn't curly-curly, despite the earlier torture, but it fell into gentle waves that wafted about her face as she walked.

Unlike the other bridesmaids, she wore only a little makeup, just enough so that her face didn't get lost in all the pink.

She was the most beautiful woman in the wedding party—maybe in the whole church. She easily outshone the bride, despite Marisa's best efforts to be the top princess. Roark studied Priscilla all through the ceremony. She didn't sniffle or dab at her eyes as the other bridesmaids did, and her face appeared almost carved in marble. But Roark could sense emotions playing just beneath the surface as she witnessed the nuptials. She would never tip her hand as to what she was feeling, but she gave off clues.

Earlier, Priscilla had told Roark not to bother waiting for her at the church; she would be delayed by endless wedding photos. He could go downtown to the reception at the Fairmont Hotel and hang out there, and she would catch a ride with someone in the wedding party.

But was that any way for a devoted, besotted boyfriend to act? He decided to stick around and watch the photographer do his thing. He couldn't get enough of watching Priscilla in this alien environment. She looked almost like a different person and not the rough-and-tumble firefighter he knew.

He caught her eye a couple of times, and she made shooing motions with her hands, indicating he should do as he was told.

He didn't budge. A real boyfriend, someone good enough to snag Priscilla, would not behave like a trained seal. Her family would see through him immediately.

An older man in a tux scooted into the pew next to Roark. "She's quite something, isn't she? My little girl." The man smiled and held out his hand. "Win Garner, Priscilla's father. I understand you're the fella who turned my girl's head."

"Roark Epperson." Roark took the other man's hand, wincing slightly at the firm handshake.

Win nodded toward the altar, where the photographer was arranging a group photo of the entire wedding party. "Make you nervous watching all this?"

"No, sir, not really." It didn't. He wasn't antimarriage, despite the failure of his first foray into matrimony. He'd seen too many good, strong marriages to have a bias against happily ever after.

He'd stood by as his parents drew strength from each other during his brother Joe's slow recovery after he was injured in a fire. He'd seen how love had triumphed over tragedy when his sister Dawn had suffered a miscarriage. He'd rejoiced when his brother Jake and his wife, Marion, had weathered every hurdle and setback imaginable in their quest to adopt their first child.

He wanted that kind of relationship. He wanted what his brothers and sisters and parents had.

He was already thirty-five. If he wanted to start a family, it was getting to be time.

"Don't let Priscilla's mother scare you," Win said. "She's already talking wedding dates—not to Priscilla, mind you, but to anyone else."

"She seems like a very nice lady," Roark said, because

what else could he say? "I'm sure she only wants Priscilla to be happy."

"That's true. Priscilla's not as strong as she appears, and on top of that she's been hurt."

The ex-boyfriend again. Who was this jerk and what had he done to her?

"I hope you'll handle her heart gently," Win concluded.

"I'll do my best." Not that Priscilla was letting him anywhere near her heart. Maybe he should ask Priscilla about this jackass of an ex-boyfriend. If she told Roark what the guy had done to hurt her, he would at least know where the minefields were.

"Good to meet ya," Win concluded with another bone-crushing handshake. "I hope you catch that arsonist fella you've been after. Let's share a brandy and cigars sometime soon, and I'll tell you all Priscilla's embarrassing stories that she keeps hoping I'll forget." With that, he got up and strolled out of the church as if he owned the place.

Priscilla approached Roark a few minutes later, slightly flushed from standing under hot photographer's lights. "I'm done. We can go now. Why didn't you go on to the reception? This must have been really tedious for you."

"No, it was interesting, actually. Your father introduced himself."

Priscilla put a hand to her forehead. "Oh, God. I meant to warn you about that. Did he give you the 'handle her heart gently' speech?"

"That was the one."

"He's given it to every guy who's ever gone out with me—at least the ones he knew about and managed to meet. He thinks I'm some delicate little flower that needs protecting, but it's his weird way of letting me know he loves me."

"So you're not still recovering from a broken heart?"

That brought her up short. "Did he say that?"

"He said you'd been hurt, that's all."

She gave an exasperated sigh. "I never had a broken heart. I was ticked off at a guy. But I'm over it now."

He wanted to know more, but a warning look in her eye stopped him from pursuing the matter. However, he didn't think she was really over it. Whatever "it" was.

THE RECEPTION, IN A chandelier-bedecked ballroom at the Fairmont, was in full swing by the time Priscilla and Roark arrived. She'd hoped they could just blend into the crowd for a while. She wasn't up to socializing with the wedding party and enduring more awkward questions about Roark.

As it turned out, though, they had chairs reserved for them among a grouping of tables intended for the wedding party and their guests. Lorraine spotted them and practically trotted over to greet them, all smiles.

"Where have you two been?" she chided gently. "You missed the bride and groom's first waltz."

"We were stuck in traffic again," Priscilla fibbed. In actuality, she'd asked Roark to drive around aimlessly with the windows open for a few minutes so she could decompress from all the frivolity.

She was genuinely happy for Marisa. But she couldn't escape the thought that not so long ago Priscilla had envisioned herself as the happy bride. She and Cory hadn't been officially engaged, but she'd known he was going to propose to her. He'd referred more than once to their future together. She'd already been thinking about the wedding to come—the colors, the food, the invitations. She'd been so shocked after the breakup that she'd never really mourned the wedding that wasn't going to happen.

It seemed a silly, girlish thing now, to feel sad because it was her cousin marrying instead of her. If her fellow firefighters knew, they would probably laugh. But the feelings were there.

"Well, you're here now," Lorraine said brightly, directing them to their assigned chairs at a table for ten. Priscilla's parents, her grandparents and a couple of stray bridesmaids and groomsmen completed the seating arrangements. "Win, get the kids some champagne."

"I'll do it," Roark said. "Would anyone else like anything?"

No one did. Before heading for the champagne fountain, Roark shot Priscilla his best basset hound look, and she tried not to laugh. If he was overdoing the besotted boyfriend routine, it was her fault.

Priscilla's gaze couldn't help but follow him as he made his way through the crowd, angling those broad shoulders. He cut a dashing figure, that was for sure. Every female he passed did a double take.

Even her grandmother was watching him. "I think you snagged yourself a hot one this time," she said. "So polite. Not cocky like that Cory."

"Mother," Lorraine said in a warning tone, shaking her head.

Priscilla braced herself for the unpleasant ping in her chest she usually felt at the mention of Cory's name. But she realized that the memory of him had lost some of its sting; she was able to let it go more easily than usual.

Roark returned with the champagne, as well as a plate with an assortment of hors d'oeuvres. "I thought you might be hungry." He set down the food, then handed one of the glasses to her. Their fingers brushed, and he slid one finger up her bare arm before sitting down. She quickly drained half the glass of cold, dry champagne, acutely aware of Roark's gaze on her. She could almost feel it physically.

She couldn't bring herself to eat even though the food was clearly delectable. Her stomach was tied up in knots. She'd told Roark not to touch her, but now she wished he would do it again. She noticed the way Marisa and Peter touched each other, their mutual caring so obvious, and she ached for that intimacy.

The small orchestra had been playing a series of big-band classics, and many of the senior citizens were happily fox-trotting on the large parquet dance floor. But when the band struck up a favorite eighties dance tune, the oldsters took a break and a younger crowd swarmed onto the floor.

"Priscilla, would you like to dance?" Roark asked politely.

"Oh, I don't think…"

"Go on, Priscilla," her mother urged. "I didn't make you go to all those dance lessons for nothing."

Priscilla knew she probably shouldn't. If she spent any time in Roark's arms, she'd be a goner. But she stood as if she were in a trance and let Roark take her hand.

The moment they hit the floor, she let him have it, deliberately driving a wedge between them. "Do you have to be so nice?"

"I can't help it," Roark said, shouting slightly over the music. "I'm a nice guy."

"I think my mother's half in love with you. My grand-mother, too."

"Even if I'm hot to trot?"

"Apparently that doesn't bother her. After you left the

dressing room, she went on and on and on about you. Having you as a fake boyfriend might be worse than having no boyfriend at all."

"Well, gee, thanks."

"No. I mean she's going to want to see more of you."

"That could be arranged."

Priscilla kicked her pink shoes to the side of the dance floor and started moving to the music, trying to feel the rhythm. But she'd only had half a glass of champagne—not enough to take the edge off her tension and loosen her muscles. "You're not honoring the spirit of our agreement."

"I'm trying."

"You're not trying hard enough. Ugh, I can't dance in this dress. It looks ridiculous."

Roark laughed. "You're right, Cinderella would not dance like that." As if he'd orchestrated it, the music abruptly changed to a slow number. The lights dropped. He wasted no time sliding one arm around her waist and taking her hand with the other. "This is more how Cinderella should dance."

Priscilla reflexively tried to back away. "No, no, no, I don't think this is a good idea." Uneasiness welled up in her chest, right along with a tendril of desire.

"Come on, Pris, I couldn't possibly hold you too close. The dress keeps me at least a foot away."

She had to laugh at that. The dress was pretty hard to maneuver around. She relaxed into the dance. This wasn't so bad. They were moving to the music, their steps matching, swaying back and forth as if they'd done this a few times before.

Still, she kept her eyes steadfastly over his shoulder and struggled to keep her breathing slow and even.

"Look at me," he said. "Who's going to believe we're crazy about each other if we don't gaze into each other's eyes during a slow song?"

He was right. She sensed her mother's eagle-eyed gaze on them, trying to discern what was really going on between her daughter and the man she was already thinking of as son-in-law material.

Priscilla forced herself to look at her partner, and her breath caught in her throat. Raw desire simmered in his dark brown eyes. An answering pang of yearning stirred in her hips, demanding attention.

He took her arms and placed them around his neck, then pulled her closer. All at once she realized he intended to kiss her. Right there in public, right on the dance floor.

"Don't…you…dare…." she said, knowing full well she did not sound as if she meant it.

Of course, he ignored her warning.

ROARK KNEW SHE DIDN'T mean it. Still, he gave her ample opportunity to escape. He moved in slowly, kissing first one corner of her mouth and then the other, alert for objections. He'd never forced himself on any woman and he didn't intend to start now.

When he sensed her compliance, he moved in for the kill. He'd been waiting for an opportunity to remind Priscilla of what they'd shared.

She responded hungrily to his kiss, clinging tightly to him as her lips came to life beneath his. He could taste the champagne on her tongue. He could feel desire seeping from her pores, which only inflamed him further.

His hand moved along the thin chiffon that covered her

back, inching toward her hip. Layers of gathered fabric prevented him from actually making contact with her skin, and at that moment all he could think of was getting that dress off her.

When someone else on the dance floor jostled him with an unintentional elbow, Roark came to his senses. The slow song was over. The lights were bright again. And he was practically molesting Priscilla in the middle of a wedding reception.

She pulled away self-consciously about the same time he did. "Roark…" she said in a strangled voice.

"Sorry," he whispered in her ear, "but only a little. Want to go somewhere?"

She started to nod, then abruptly stopped herself. "Leaving this early would be rude."

Roark refused to be discouraged. She hadn't said no, which opened up possibilities for later, when they could depart without raising eyebrows.

He coaxed Priscilla into a few more dances and held her hand or touched the small of her back whenever they weren't on the dance floor—just so she wouldn't lose track of the connection they'd made. He was definitely violating her no-contact mandate, but she didn't object. He suffered through speeches and cake-cutting, all the while wondering when he could get her alone.

Finally it was time for Marisa to throw her bouquet. Roark watched with quiet amusement as Lorraine dragged her recalcitrant daughter into the crowd of single women, determined that Priscilla would catch the flowers.

As the bouquet sailed toward her, Priscilla kept her arms at her side and a more willing girl made the catch.

When Priscilla rejoined Roark, she burst out laughing,

then quickly stifled her mirth. "Oh, my God, that was classic. Could Mother have been any more transparent?"

"I'm flattered your mother likes me that much. Not too sure about your father, though. He's been glaring at me." He probably didn't like Roark kissing his little girl on the dance floor.

"He doesn't want you to think he's a pushover."

A few minutes later Marisa and Peter made their farewells and left in a flurry of hugs and a shower of rice.

"Is it okay for us to leave now?" Roark asked.

Priscilla gave him a challenging look. "I hadn't realized you were so anxious for the evening to end."

"You know I'm not. I'm just tired of sharing you with a roomful of people."

If she was going to object, now would be the time. For a moment she hesitated. Then she looked away and made quick work of saying her good-nights. Roark hoped that Win Garner couldn't read his mind as he shook the older man's hand, but he felt as if it was tattooed on his forehead. He wanted Priscilla—if not in his bed, at least in his arms.

Finally they were alone in the elevator, and Roark wondered if there was any way to recapture the sensuality they'd found for themselves on the dance floor. He smoothed a strand of hair from her cheek and tucked it behind her ear. She looked at him, her eyes full of questions.

"I want to take you home with me," he said.

Her chin jutted out. "That's not in the game plan."

"I think it's time for a new game plan."

She didn't agree, but she didn't come out and say no, either. She looked decidedly worried.

When a valet pulled the car around, Roark again helped

Priscilla get situated in the passenger seat, stuffing the enormous skirts of her unruly dress inside and shutting the door before it could escape.

He tipped the valet and slid behind the wheel.

Priscilla was ready for him. "Maybe we should just go back to my house."

If it was any other woman, he might take that as an invitation. But he knew what Priscilla meant. She wanted him to take her home and leave her there—alone. Was there anything he could say or do to change her mind?

Roark meandered his way toward Oak Cliff. After crossing the Houston Street bridge, he turned left at the entrance to Lake Cliff Park. It was a small, heavily wooded park, dark and deserted this evening.

Priscilla suddenly realized Roark had strayed from her intended trajectory. "Where are we going?"

He pulled up next to the curb and stopped. "Can we go back to what happened during that first slow dance? We were on the same wavelength then. I wanted to be alone with you, and you wanted the same thing—even if your good manners got in the way."

She plastered her back against the far door. "I wasn't thinking straight."

"Is it so important to think straight all the time?"

"Not all the time. Just around you."

"Because you don't want to lose control."

"Because things *will* get out of hand. You know they will. Look what happened on the dance floor. All you have to do is touch me, and my good sense flies right out the window." She folded her arms, causing her breasts to swell above the neckline of the gown.

Maybe it wasn't such a bad dress after all. "We're in a

car," Roark argued reasonably. "A Porsche, which isn't exactly conducive to wild sex. And we're in a public place. Things can't get that out of hand. Besides, you're wearing the pink chiffon equivalent of a chastity belt."

With that comment, he actually coaxed a smile out of her.

"I'm not going to ravish you against your will. That's not my style."

"Of course you won't. You won't have to."

Seeing that she really was distressed about the idea that she might get carried away by her hormones, he took pity. No reason to rush her. He didn't just want sex with Priscilla, anyway. He wasn't yet sure what he wanted, but it was definitely more than a roll in the hay.

"Let's just talk then." He leaned his seat back, released his seat belt and folded his arms behind his head

"About what?" she asked, full of suspicion.

"Anything you want. Why don't you tell me what you and Marisa did when you were little girls. Did you play with dolls?"

"Me? No. I had a fleet of Tonka trucks." She inched away from the door some.

Roark laughed. "You're making this up."

"I'm not. Marisa had dolls and stuffed animals. I had trucks and LEGOs. We still managed to play together, though I'm not sure how."

"LEGOs. My brother and I used to build huge castles with those things."

"Just one brother? Don't you have a bunch?"

"I have three, but Joe and I were closest in age. He's about to have a kid of his own now."

Priscilla pushed her seat back even with his. "So you'll be Uncle Roark."

"Oh, I'm already Uncle Roark. Eleven times over."

"Wow. Do you get to see your family often?"

"Not as often as I'd like. They're all in and around Boston. I moved to Texas because Libby's family was here. By the time we split up, I was already firmly entrenched in the Dallas fire department, so I stayed. But sometimes it's hard being so far from them."

"Family's important. I complain about mine, but I wouldn't want to move too far from them."

A night bird called in the trees and another answered. It was a lonely sound. Roark reached for Priscilla's hand and entwined his fingers with hers. This time when he squeezed, she squeezed back.

His face was only a few inches from hers. Roark wasn't sure whether he'd moved toward her or if she was the one who'd come closer. Maybe they'd both leaned in. But another kiss was just a breath away.

Her gaze flickered down to his mouth and back again.

Their lips met, but this time there was no crowd of onlookers. They were alone in a car on a dark street. The windows were already fogged up.

Everything Roark had said was true—the car's cramped confines made sex nearly impossible, and to try and get Priscilla out of the pink dress would be to invite serious injury. But that didn't stop him from immediately wondering whether it could be done.

He controlled himself. He *had* to. He was not going to give this woman one reason to pull back or let her fears take over. He was totally committed to letting her set the pace.

Her breasts were tempting, but he resisted. Instead he touched her face, running one finger along her jaw, then buried his hand in her hair.

Suddenly she tensed. "What is that noise?"

Talk about bad timing. "It's…my phone." Set on vibrate. With no small regret, Roark pulled away from Priscilla and reached into his jacket pocket for his cell.

"You're not actually going to answer that, are you?"

He checked the caller ID. His heart sank. "I have to. It's the alarm office. They wouldn't call me unless it was an emergency." He opened the phone. "Epperson. This better be good."

"Sorry to spoil your evening, Captain. We got a blaze going in an empty apartment building in South Dallas. The IC says it bears all the earmarks of your arsonist." The dispatcher rattled off an address. "You know it?"

"I can find it." He had a GPS locator in his car. "I'll come right now."

"The warehouse arsonist?" Priscilla asked when he'd disconnected. She'd already straightened her seat.

He nodded. "And when I find the son of a bitch, I'm going to kill him."

Chapter Five

Recovering from the kiss, Priscilla looked down to make sure she was still decently covered by her clothes. Other times they'd been together, her clothing had seemed to magically disappear. But this time her dress was perfectly in place.

Roark might be angry over the interruption, but she was actually grateful. Grateful for the chance to reevaluate this situation. When Roark had stopped his car in the deserted park, Priscilla had been adamant that nothing would happen. But he'd easily disarmed her with nothing more than a quiet conversation.

She couldn't even blame him for initiating the kiss, because she was the one who'd leaned in first. So much for her backbone.

"I gather you're not taking me home first," she said.

"No time. I've got to get to the fire as quick as I can." He turned on the engine, returned his seat to its normal position and entered the address of the fire into his GPS unit. "I'm sorry, Priscilla. I know this is really rude."

"I understand. I want this guy caught, too. Can I tag along? Watch you work?"

"You can do more than that. There's a video camera in

the glove box. If you could record the fire and especially the onlookers, it would help a great deal."

"Sure, I can do that." She was amazed by how quickly she was able to switch gears. A minute earlier, desire had caused her blood to rush through her veins. Now her heart was pumping at high speed for an entirely different reason.

A fire always had that effect. But a fire set by the serial arsonist—she couldn't wait to see it. She wanted a crack at this guy.

She reached behind the seat and retrieved one of her bags containing the clothes she'd worn to the church. "I'll have to change. I can hardly tromp around a fire in this. If a cinder landed on this skirt, I'd go up like a Roman candle." While Roark drove, she shimmied into her jeans and sneakers.

Thanks to Roark's lead foot, they arrived in well under the eight minutes the GPS had estimated. They stopped a couple of blocks short of the fire ground, behind engines and ladder trucks, police cruisers and other official vehicles.

"Unzip me." She turned her back toward him as he opened his door.

"What? Oh." He ran the zipper down, baring her back from neck to hips. "I wish this was under different circumstances."

She shivered. "Close the door. I'll be out in two seconds." Thankful for tinted glass, Priscilla shed the dress and pulled on her shirt, trying not to think about the feel of his fingers brushing her back. Moments later she grabbed the video camera from the glove box and joined Roark as he dug through the trunk, where he kept a set of turnout gear.

As soon as he was suited up, they walked closer to the fire. Roark flashed his badge at anyone who looked as if he might question their presence.

The small apartment building was entirely engulfed in flames. Even Priscilla, who didn't have the world's most sensitive nose, could smell gasoline—the serial arsonist's accelerant of choice.

"This is close enough for you," Roark said, stopping well away from the action.

"But—"

"No buts. At this fire, you're officially a citizen, not a firefighter."

"Okay," she agreed, though grudgingly. He was right. Her thin shirt would provide no protection against blowing embers. She hated being left out of the action, but without her fire gear she would be a liability rather than a help. She turned on the video camera and started recording, paying special attention to the onlookers, as Roark had requested.

And there were a lot of them. What better way to spend a Saturday night than to watch something burn?

"Hey," someone called out. "Take my picture, lady!"

She turned toward the voice and discovered a group of teenage boys wearing gang colors. She obliged them by turning the camera on them. They mugged for her, flexing their muscles, making gang signs, waving and saying hi to their mothers.

The arsonist probably was not a gang member. Roark thought he was someone a bit older, someone with knowledge of firefighting if not actual experience.

"There's a big reward if you can tell the police who started this fire," she told the kids just in case.

"Hey, even if we knew," one of the boys said, "we wouldn't tell *you*." They ambled away.

Priscilla alternated between recording the fire itself and the onlookers. She didn't stay where Roark had parked her, but she didn't invite trouble by getting any closer to the action, either. She wandered around, aiming the camera at various knots of glassy-eyed neighbors and kids who ought to be home in bed, tough-looking young men swilling beer, even police officers who'd heard the call go out and had come to watch and assist if needed.

Support staff from the fire department had arrived with a van full of bottled water, snacks and cool, wet towels.

Blue-Lighters were arriving, too—they were like moths, attracted to any flame. They listened to their scanners 24/7 and drove like crazy to any fire that sounded worthwhile, their cars often equipped with the flashing blue lights— strictly unofficial—that gave the group its name. These en- thusiastic citizens were intrigued by all fire and police activities, but often they were in the way and sometimes they hindered operations.

Priscilla got them on video. Although generally suppor- tive, they loved fires, and any of them could be an arsonist.

She recorded Roark as he worked. He shone a flash- light inside the front door—up, down, side to side. And then he stepped inside, where the worst danger was likely to be concealed.

Priscilla's heart was in her throat. The fire was definitely under control now and Roark knew what he was doing, but she still couldn't bear it if something happened to him— or to anyone, she quickly amended.

To take her mind off the danger, she returned to com- mitting the onlookers to videotape.

One spectator in particular caught her attention. He was a young guy, maybe late twenties, scruffy-looking, dark hair, wearing a black zip-up sweatshirt and a Blue-Lighter baseball cap. He stood alone just a few feet from her, frozen, staring, mesmerized by the fire, a slight smile playing about his face.

The smile gave Priscilla the creeps. Not only that, but the guy looked familiar to her. She was almost positive she had met him somewhere before, but she couldn't place when or where. She raised the camera to get him on tape, but the second she did he turned and walked away.

Roark strode back out only a few short seconds later and yanked off his breathing apparatus. His face was tight and angry. He spoke a few words to the Incident Commander, and whatever he'd said disturbed the IC. Then the IC raised his bullhorn.

"Code red, code red. All personnel, evacuate and clear this area immediately."

Code red. That could mean only one thing—a serious threat to life and limb for anyone in the vicinity.

ROARK COULD NOT BELIEVE how close he'd just come to death. The arsonist had set up a pipe bomb with a trip wire—a more sophisticated detonating method than the previous bomb, which had been on a timer that hadn't worked. If Roark had taken one more step, the shrapnel from the bomb would have cut him into a million pieces.

But he'd happened to shine his flashlight right on the device. Then he'd seen the trip wire.

He scanned the crowd for Priscilla and breathed a quiet sigh of relief when he spotted her. She was urging onlookers to move back as police set up barricades. He wondered if anyone took her seriously, then decided they probably did. Her delicate, feminine appearance notwithstanding, if she wanted to get her point across, she could. Fiercely.

The Dallas bomb squad had been called in, and until they arrived and deactivated the bomb, there was nothing Roark could do. He made his way to Priscilla.

"I'm sorry about all this," Roark said, looking around. "I'm going to be here for a while—until daylight, at least. Why don't you take my car home and call it a night?"

"You'd let me drive your Porsche?"

"If there's anything left of it. This isn't the best neighborhood." This part of South Dallas was nothing but boarded-up buildings, rusty chain-link fences, abandoned cars and weedy lots. The street was littered with beer bottles and other trash, and every vertical surface bore gang graffiti.

"All right," she said, sounding disappointed, which was somewhat gratifying. At least she wasn't looking for any excuse to get away from him. They started walking toward where he'd parked his car, and Priscilla stopped. "Oh, wait. There's this guy I want you to look at. The way he was watching the fire, standing all alone and sort of smiling— it was really creepy."

She looked all around, then looked again. "I don't see him now. But I got him on tape. He's a Blue-Lighter."

"Then I can probably get an ID on him through Betty." Betty was the self-appointed leader and organizer of the group and she was always willing to help.

They resumed walking toward the Porsche, which was parked where Roark had left it and appeared to be intact. Thank God for small favors.

He pulled the keys out of his pocket. "You can drive a stick, right?"

"What do I look like, a girlie girl?"

He pretended to study her critically. "Kind of smudged up at the moment, but definitely girlie."

"I can drive a stick."

He still didn't give her the keys. He backed her up against the side of the car and put a hand on either side of her, trapping her. "This was about the most memorable date I've ever had."

"Memorable. Is that good?"

"Definitely good. I'll come get the car tomorrow. We'll talk."

"There's nothing to talk about." Her gaze skittered away from his guiltily.

"I disagree. You're not going to hold me to this fictional boyfriend crap, are you?"

"No, actually. I'm going to have to fictionally break up with you. Otherwise my mother will be reserving the church and ordering flowers."

"Tell her to cut it out. You're not exactly a shrinking violet."

"Oh, Roark, don't you see? This really has nothing to do with my mother. You make me completely crazy. If that call hadn't come on your cell, no telling where all that kissing would have taken us, but it would have been somewhere against my better judgment. I don't want to be like that. I like having control over my life. And around you…I just lose it."

He couldn't argue with that. She could be a wildcat when she was aroused. "I would try, really hard, not to let anything bad happen to you. I wish you'd trust me."

"I do trust you. Really, I do. But I have to look out for myself. I'm not ready for anything heavy at this point in my life."

Lame excuse if he ever heard one. "I didn't take you for a coward."

"When it comes to burning buildings, no. When it comes

to my personal life…yeah. Maybe. Frankly, I'm not sure why anyone who's survived a nasty breakup would want to jump back into a relationship."

Maybe she had a point. It had taken him ten years. But this was a discussion that would take some time, and these weren't the best circumstances.

He kissed Priscilla on the forehead and handed her the keys. "We'll talk," he said again. He was not giving up on her. Surrender was not an option.

ROARK WAS EXHAUSTED by the time a police officer dropped him off at his loft the next morning. The stress of pitting his wits against the serial arsonist was beginning to take its toll.

Normally Roark found his loft a soothing, restful place to shake off the stresses of the day—or, in this case, the night. During his divorce, he and Libby had sold the little two-bedroom dollhouse they'd bought in an old East Dallas neighborhood. He'd decided to move somewhere completely different, and an urban loft in Oak Lawn had captured his imagination.

The space, located over a row of quirky retail shops, had given him something to do with his time. He'd refinished the rough plank floors, removed plaster to expose the original red brick and installed a sleek industrial-looking kitchen. The only room actually closed off was a bath; everything else was left open, with only one wall of glass block demarcating the bedroom. The furnishings were streamlined and modern—nothing the slightest bit "homey."

It had suited him at the time, and he still liked the clean, uncluttered lines, though at this point in his life a woman's touch would not be unwelcome.

This morning, his comfortable home surroundings didn't relax him at all. So instead of going to bed, Roark downloaded the video footage from his camera onto his computer and watched the sequences Priscilla had recorded. Maybe he could spot something, some clue that would help him catch the arsonist.

If he didn't get a break soon, the guy was going to succeed in killing more firefighters. The bomb squad had informed Roark that the device hidden inside the burning building would have killed him if he'd tripped the wire.

A guy in a black nylon jacket popped up on the screen. Was this the weird guy Priscilla had mentioned? But he was only visible for a second, and the quality of the video wasn't very good in the low light.

"Sorry I couldn't get a better shot," Priscilla said. "He's wearing a Blue-Lighter cap, in case you can't see it clearly." The sound of her taped voice sent a pleasurable shiver up Roark's spine. He played that portion of the recording again, then a third time. But after that he made himself stop. He had an arsonist to catch, an arsonist who liked playing dangerous games. The next fire, it could be Priscilla who entered a burning building and ended up a statistic.

He wouldn't be able to bear the guilt, not a second time. When he was eighteen, he'd nearly lost his own little brother in a dormitory fire—an arson fire—at their boarding school. Seven boys had suffered injuries. His own brother's had been the most serious. Joe hadn't been expected to live.

He had lived, though. He bore horrible scars and he would be in a wheelchair the rest of his life. But he'd gone on to live a productive life. He was an assistant district attorney in Boston, with a beautiful wife and his first baby on the way.

That didn't stop Roark from feeling the guilt every time he saw Joe sitting in his chair, his face and hands covered in scar tissue. Though he'd only been a teenager himself, Roark had always felt he could have done *something* to save his brother, if only he'd reacted quicker or moved faster.

Obviously Roark could not change history, no matter how many arsonists he took off the street. But that didn't stop him from trying.

Impulsively he picked up the phone and called Joe on his cell.

"Hey, bro." Joe's voice was easy, congenial. He was probably busy—he was always busy. But he was never too busy to at least touch base. "What's going on?"

"The serial arsonist struck again," Roark said. "No one hurt this time, thank God." He went on to detail the night's events. "I have a possible suspect on video. Can I send you a clip? Maybe you can give me a read on this guy." Joe had the keenest instincts when it came to reading a suspect's facial expressions and body language.

"Sure, send it on. Who took the video?"

"My date."

"Priscilla?"

"Yeah." Last time they'd talked, Roark had filled Joe in on the unconventional arrangements he'd made to pretend to be Priscilla's boyfriend.

"You took her on a date…to a fire? You sure know how to show a girl a good time."

"I was on call. Anyway, she wanted to come with me."

"So how did it go other than that?"

Roark realized then why he'd called his brother, and it wasn't strictly because of the arsonist. He needed to vent his frustration to someone, but he couldn't talk about Priscilla to anyone at work. Although there were no official bans on Dallas Fire-Rescue employees dating each other, he didn't want to encourage gossip.

"I don't understand this woman at all," Roark blurted out. "Not even remotely. I've taken all kinds of psychology classes, read a million books on human behavior and I still don't get her. We have chemistry, we have common interests, we like each other. Even her mother likes me. But Priscilla refuses to consider…you know…moving things along."

"But you've slept with her."

"That was months ago. I'm telling you, something doesn't feel quite right. I mean, yeah, some guy dumped her last year. But she's not a fragile little flower. She's tough and practical and pragmatic—not the type to obsess over an ex-boyfriend."

"She's a woman. She has hormones men don't understand. Believe me, I know all about hormones. Danni has become the most illogical person I've ever known."

Danni was Joe's very pregnant wife. "Is she doing all right?"

"Physically she's perfect. She looks like an adorable…walrus. But she's an emotional wreck." Joe laughed. "Yesterday, she lost it over the way I cut up a tomato for a salad."

Roark laughed, too. He'd heard a lot of pregnancy anecdotes from his siblings over the years—cravings, temper tantrums and crazed trips to the hospital for delivery—and they never failed to amuse him.

"Give her my love."

"I will. But let's get back to Priscilla. What are you going to do about her?"

"I'm going to figure out what it is she's not telling me. I won't know what to do until I have all the facts."

"And then?"

Roark let out a long breath. "I haven't a clue."

"SO, HOW WAS THE WEDDING?" Tony asked Priscilla the next day when she wandered downstairs to retrieve the newspaper. Tony, Ethan and their families were getting ready to head out to a tailgate party at Texas Stadium, followed by a Cowboys game. Priscilla had been invited to go, too, but she'd declined. It wasn't that she didn't enjoy football, but she *was* starting to feel like an extraneous limb. Her two best friends were all about family now. And since she didn't have a family of her own, she didn't really fit in.

"The wedding was fine." She headed out the front door, hoping to avoid an interrogation.

Tony followed her out. "Fine? Appears to me like things worked out more than just fine." And he looked pointedly at the driveway, where Roark's Porsche gleamed in the morning sun.

"Oh. It's not what it looks like. Roark's car is here, but he's not. He got called to a fire last night." And to make her point, she pulled the newspaper out of its plastic bag and unfurled it to the front page. Sure enough, the headline was "Arsonist strikes again." A color picture ran across four columns showing the conflagration in all its glory.

Tony immediately sobered. "Was anyone hurt?"

"I don't think so. But, Tony, there was another bomb."

Tony slapped the newspaper against his thigh. "We've got to catch this guy." Although no one mentioned how much more dangerous this guy made all their jobs, it was in the back of everyone's minds.

Ethan, who was loading a cooler into the back of his SUV, overheard and wandered over. "I heard about the fire." He peered around Tony to look at the paper. "Were you there, Pris?"

"Yeah. In fact…" She looked more closely at the picture, then pointed. "That's me. The blue speck way off in the corner."

"Man, ole Epperson knows how to show a girl a good time."

"The wedding was over. He was taking me home when he got the call." She left out any mention of the detour they'd taken to a park before they'd even known about the fire.

"Did Roark play his part?" Ethan asked.

She sighed. "If you must know, Roark did such a stellar job that my mother already has us married off in her mind. She'll be heartbroken when I tell her Roark and I split up."

"You split up?" Tony asked, sounding troubled by the idea.

"Tony, get a grip. It was a fictional relationship, so I can fictionally break it up if I need to." Except it didn't feel fictional. She'd replayed her last conversation with Roark over and over as she'd driven his car home, then had lain awake unable to sleep, punching her pillow and wondering what was wrong with her that she couldn't have a normal relationship with a guy most women would amputate a leg to go out with.

Was she still mourning her breakup with Cory? It didn't feel as though that was the case. Her logical side told her she was lucky to have escaped marriage to a guy who would dump a woman because she couldn't have children. Yet she simply couldn't bring herself to move forward with Roark.

It had to be the control issue. When she dated a guy, she liked to be the one calling the shots. She'd never felt out of control with Cory—not until that very last day.

With Roark, she would never call the shots. Her attempts at a "game plan" had failed miserably. She'd already proved she couldn't control him *or* herself.

"Are you sure it's fictional?" Ethan asked, nodding toward the Porsche.

"Oh, for heaven's sake, do I have to explain this again? Roark got called to the fire. He was going to be there all night, so he sent me home in his car."

"He let you drive his Porsche?" Tony asked, obviously skeptical.

"Why wouldn't he? I'm a good driver."

Ethan tried to stifle a snort.

"Oh, yeah, just because I hit a barricade the first time I drove the ambulance. You weren't there, and that story got blown way out of proportion. I nudged the barricade, that's all." She was more than happy to shift the discussion away from her and Roark. She let the two friends tease her about her driving. She didn't mind, because if anyone else gave her trouble, they would stick up for her.

The others left for the stadium, and Priscilla put some frozen pancakes in the microwave. She hadn't eaten since lunch yesterday and she was starving. As she waited for the microwave to ding, she turned on the TV and searched the news channels to see if there was any mention of the fire.

The doorbell rang before her pancakes were ready, and she tensed, knowing who it was. Roark had come to collect his car and he needed his keys. She went to get them from the umbrella stand—where she was sure she'd left them the previous night—but they were nowhere to be found.

She couldn't leave Roark standing on the front porch while she searched, so she ran down the stairs barefoot and opened the door, bracing herself for her reaction to him. Roark was dressed in faded jeans and a navy corduroy shirt, obviously fresh from a shower. His hair was still slightly damp around the edges.

But he hadn't shaved, which surprised her. She'd never seen him anything but perfectly groomed.

"Is everything okay?" she asked.

"No, actually, things pretty much suck. A lunatic is trying to turn Dallas firefighters into mincemeat, and I can't stop him. And the woman I'm crazy about won't see me. Things aren't really going my way right now. But I won't bore you with details. Can I have my keys?"

"Roark, don't hate me."

"I don't hate you. I just told you I'm crazy about you. I just don't want to make things more difficult than they already are."

She didn't think she could feel worse about how she'd handled things, but somehow there was always a new level of wretchedness she could sink to. "Your keys are upstairs…somewhere. Come on up."

He followed her wordlessly up the flight of stairs. But when she opened the door, he stopped in the doorway and stared.

"Pink?"

She'd almost forgotten her walls were pink, she was so used to ignoring the color. "You think this is bad, you should have seen the place before I started redecorating. My mother thought that since I was spending so much time with men, I needed a thoroughly feminine place to come home to. She surprised me with a while-you-were-out makeover. This place was so crowded with lace and ruffles and cabbage roses it would have nauseated Laura Ashley."

She flipped back the cream-colored slipcover on her sofa to reveal floral chintz upholstery, then quickly covered it up.

Gradually she'd been replacing the fussy furnishings with more modern pieces. She'd taken down the curtains to better display the retro venetian blinds, and the flowery throw rugs had given way to floor coverings with innocuous geometric patterns. The walls were now mostly bare except for one modern painting she'd bought from a street artist. The bright colors ensured her living room wouldn't be *too* bland.

"I'm going to repaint," she said. "I just haven't had time."

"What color will you change it to?"

She gave him a puzzled look. "Why do you want to know?"

He shrugged. "Just curious."

"Off-white, I guess."

He nodded, seeming satisfied with her answer.

"I'll just get those keys…." But she couldn't find them. They weren't in the dish on the umbrella stand. And they weren't on the dining room table.

They weren't in her purse or in any of the shopping bags she'd brought in from the car last night.

"Maybe they're in the bedroom." She darted through a doorway, hoping Roark wouldn't follow her. But he did. He stared at the bed as she searched the floor, the bedside table and the bookshelf.

Finally, in desperation, she stripped back the cream silk duvet and groped around under the pillows. What had she done with the damn keys?

"You're killing me, you know."

"You didn't have to follow me in here," she snapped, scrambling off the bed before he got any ideas. Any *more* ideas. Had she subconsciously hidden the keys from herself to prolong her contact with Roark?

"What's that smell?" he asked.

She sniffed but couldn't detect anything unusual. "Does it smell like maple syrup?"

"Yeah." He took a deep breath and closed his eyes.

"It's frozen microwave pancakes." She took pity on him. He looked hungry. "I can make extra."

"I'm starving," he admitted. "My kitchen is about as bare as it's ever been."

She headed for her own tiny kitchen. Roark followed her as far as the living room, where the TV snagged his attention. "Did we make CNN?"

"I don't know, I'd just turned on the TV when the doorbell rang," she called to him from the kitchen. A few moments later she set the pancakes on the coffee table in front of Roark. "I'll join you in a minute. We can watch the news." Something nice and impersonal.

She popped a second set of pancakes in the microwave, and while they were heating she poured two mugs of coffee. She returned to the living room to find Roark passed out on her sofa, one of her throw pillows scrunched under his head. His pancakes were untouched.

She didn't have the heart to wake him. This investigation was obviously wearing him down. She covered him with a blanket and then couldn't resist gently smoothing his hair off his forehead, barely touching him so he wouldn't wake up. He looked almost boyish like this, his face relaxed. Normally he was so intense—even when he was making love.

Especially when he was making love.

She tried not to let her mind stray there. Dangerous territory.

Priscilla ate one stack of pancakes, then wrapped up the others for another time. Roark was still snoozing peacefully, so she decided this was a good time to find his keys. She knew she hadn't locked them in the car, knew they had to be in this apartment somewhere.

After another fifteen minutes she finally found them— in the kitchen, on the counter near the fridge. She remembered now, she'd gone in there to get a drink of water before she'd gone to bed.

Roark still didn't move.

She went into her tiny second bedroom, which she'd set up with a desk and computer for her paramedic training. She had one more computer module to watch before her next live class.

The paramedic training was getting more interesting as the weeks passed. Priscilla and Ethan were now qualified as Emergency Medical Technicians, the first step toward paramedic certification. They'd survived their emergency-room and ambulance rotations and passed their qualifying exams, which allowed them to do patient assessment and some noninvasive medical procedures—like splinting broken bones and CPR.

Now they were learning more advanced patient care, like inserting IVs, drawing blood and intubation. Although Priscilla had gone into the fire service because she liked the idea of putting out fires and carrying out daring rescues, she'd been on enough medical emergencies to know that she also liked that aspect of her work.

Two hours later, she'd completed the module *and*

taken the online practice test, passing it with ease. She stretched—then remembered she had a sexy six-foot visitor lying on her sofa. She went to the living room to check on him. He was still dead to the world, though he had shifted to a more comfortable-looking position.

She decided she had better wake him up. What if he was supposed to be somewhere? She was pretty sure he hadn't intended to spend the entire day on her sofa. She gingerly touched his shoulder.

"Roark?"

He didn't move.

She jostled him. "Roark?" She spoke more emphatically this time. Good gravy, the man slept like the dead.

"Roark!"

This time his eyes flew open. "What?" He sat up, looking around him in a pure fight-or-flight response until his eyes settled on Priscilla. "What happened?"

"You fell asleep. I went to make you pancakes and when I came back you were unconscious."

He looked at his watch. "Oh, jeez. I've been asleep for two hours?"

"I'd have let you sleep longer—you look like you need it. But I was afraid you might have other plans."

He rubbed his eyes. "Nothing pressing. Sorry, Pris. You're probably ready to be rid of me by now."

"You weren't bothering me. In fact, you can nap some more if you want. You look exhausted."

"Thanks, but I think I'll get on home. Did you find my keys?"

It was so tempting to tell him she hadn't. But that was just pure perversity on her part—dragging out their time together when she was the one who'd declared they couldn't see each other. She picked up his keys from the coffee table and handed them to him. "Sorry I misplaced them." Sorry for everything, including the kink he would have in his back from sleeping on her too-short sofa.

He took the keys but remained seated. "Priscilla, is there something you're not telling me?"

"What do you mean?"

"I just get this feeling you haven't put all your playing pieces on the board."

She didn't like this line of questioning. Yes, she did have a few secrets. But she wasn't obliged to spill them—to anyone. On the other hand, Roark was a skilled interrogator. If he was determined to find something out, he could do it.

Earlier, she'd been questioning her decision to stay away from Roark. But now she remembered why she had to do just that. This man had the ability to lay her bare. And that meant he also had the capacity to crush her—far more thoroughly than Cory had.

She put her hands on her hips. "Why can't you just take no for an answer?"

"Because I did that once before. I accepted that my marriage was over without really knowing all the facts. But I've learned not to let things go without a fight."

"Some things aren't worth fighting for."

"And some things are."

They stared at each other for several tense heartbeats. "You're used to getting your way."

"I am."

"It's not going to work with me."

Another long pause as they sized each other up, challenging, searching for chinks in the armor. The only chink Priscilla saw in Roark's armor was his compassion. He wouldn't deliberately hurt her just for the sake of having his way. But she had no idea what weaknesses he saw in her.

Finally he stood. "Guess I'll be going, then."

"Roark…"

"No, you're right. You made it clear from the beginning that you weren't interested in a relationship. You asked me not to touch you. I should have respected those boundaries. I didn't. I thought I could change your mind."

He'd probably never know how close he'd come to doing just that, how close she'd come to convincing herself she could handle the intense desire and the confusing fears that swamped her every time he was near.

But she couldn't. If she'd learned one thing about herself, it was that she needed to feel as if she had some control over her world—and herself.

Priscilla walked Roark down the stairs to the front door, and then a question occurred to her. "Did you learn anything new last night about the arson? Anything you didn't tell the reporters?" She felt much more comfortable talking shop.

"I've got my team over there right now, combing every inch of the scene for evidence. But so far, nothing." He paused. "The bomb was much improved over his first attempt. The guy's getting smarter—and even more dangerous."

"You'll get him. Did you look at the video?"

"Yeah, and I saw the guy you were talking about. But his face wasn't clear enough for an ID."

"Sorry I didn't do better. He was camera-shy. But I got a good look at him. And, Roark…I know that guy from somewhere. The more I think about it, the more positive I am that I haven't just seen him in a crowd. I've spoken to him. But I can't remember when or where."

Roark seemed encouraged by her news. "Keep trying to remember. If you or Betty can ID him, I'll talk to him. But if not, I'm not sure what else I can do. It's not against the law to watch a fire with a strange look on your face."

Chapter Six

It was time to pay the piper.

Priscilla had put off telling her mother she and Roark had "broken up." But today Priscilla had agreed to go shopping with her mother to help her find a dress for the Leukemia Society Ball—Lorraine Garner was on the board of directors. Priscilla had to tell her; to let her mother go on believing she had found the love of her life was cruel.

They met at Northpark Mall, Dallas's oldest mall, and still the finest according to Lorraine. Their first stop was Neiman Marcus.

"Usually I can find something suitable here," Priscilla's mother said as she worked her way through a rack of designer evening wear. "But if not, we can try Nordstrom. Or maybe that new place, the little boutique you like."

Priscilla was a bit surprised that her mother would even consider shopping at Kiki's. The inventory there was way funkier than her usual taste.

Mrs. Garner pulled a dress from the rack, a soft beige sleeveless number with a draped neckline, almost no back and lots of sparkles. "Now this isn't bad."

"Mother, I can't believe you'd be caught dead in something like that."

The woman laughed. "Not for me, dear. But it would look wonderful on you."

"I thought we were looking for a dress for you."

"We are. But if we just happen to run across something that perfectly suits you…I mean, you need something to wear to the ball, too." When Priscilla didn't comment, her mother said, "You and Roark *are* planning to attend…right?"

Priscilla couldn't procrastinate any longer. "Mother, I know you like Roark, and I do, too, but it's just not going to work out between us."

"What? Why not?" She hung the gown back on the rack, instantly forgotten.

"I'm not ready for a serious relationship."

"Oh, honey." The older woman put her arms around Priscilla and hugged her hard. "Just because Cory was too shallow to see—"

"No, that's not it," Priscilla hastened to say, gently extricating herself from the hug. "I'm only just now figuring out who I am. I want to be…just me for a while." Priscilla Garner, girl firefighter.

Her mother waved away Priscilla's concern. "If a man truly loves you, he's going to let you be exactly who you are. He won't try to change you. True, I haven't spent much time with Roark, but I can tell he likes you just the way you are. He would accept *everything* about you. Including infertility."

Priscilla had known her mother would bring up the subject sooner or later. "The fact I can't have children has nothing to do with this. Really. The subject hasn't even come up." Suddenly she felt this compulsion to be honest. Her mother had been trying so hard to let go of attempting to control Priscilla, to honor her choices. And Priscilla felt guilty all of a sudden for having deceived her.

"Okay, so here's the deal. Roark was never my boyfriend. He agreed to *pose* as my boyfriend so you would stop worrying about me and trying to set me up with suitable guys."

The expressions that played across Lorraine's face were almost comical—anger at being lied to, then guilt over her incessant matchmaking, then plain old confusion. "If he wasn't your boyfriend, why was he kissing you like that?"

Priscilla shrugged. "It was just a spur-of-the-moment thing. He was trying to get into the role...."

"If he was just playing a role, he's the best actor I ever saw. The way you two were looking at each other..."

Priscilla silently pleaded with her mother to drop the subject.

"Priscilla, honey, good men do not grow on trees. If you let your fear of rejection stop you from even trying a new relationship, you might miss a very good opportunity."

"I don't fear rejection," she said. "I'm just not ready to turn over big chunks of my life to a guy. I want to be in the driver's seat for a while. I want to focus on my career and my training."

"And I think you're looking for excuses. A smoke screen to hide behind. Loving someone is a risk, no doubt about it. But you can't lock yourself up in a convent your whole life."

"Mother, you're making more out of this than is necessary. Roark's not right for me."

Lorraine looked unbearably sad for a moment. But she did let the subject drop. She returned her attention to shopping, but they'd both lost their enthusiasm for the outing.

Later that evening, as Priscilla drove down Northwest Highway toward the Tollway, her mother's words kept

She seemed to feel his gaze on her, because she looked up and smiled tentatively. "Hi."

"Hi. You look nice," he couldn't resist saying, even if it wasn't professional.

"Oh." She tucked a stray strand of hair behind her ear. "Thanks."

He sat next to her on the banquette and handed her the sheets of mug shots he'd printed. "Just look at each of the photos and let me know if any of them could be the wind-breaker guy. Take your time. I'll get us some coffee. You want a nonfat latte?" That was what she'd ordered that first night they'd had coffee and again at the Nodding Dog. He remembered everything about his time with her.

"That'd be nice, thanks. Uh, none of these guys are Dallas firefighters, right?"

He understood her reluctance to identify one of their own as a suspect, so he was relieved to be able to reassure her the men in these photos were all men with arson arrest records.

When he returned a couple of minutes later with their coffees, she was engrossed in studying the pictures; she murmured a thanks for her drink and sipped at it distract-edly as her gaze darted from photo to photo. Roark resisted the urge to say anything. She would tell him if any of these guys looked familiar.

Priscilla carefully studied each image. But her face registered no emotion, no hint of recognition—until she hit the last page.

Then her eyes widened and her breath quickened.

"Priscilla?"

She jumped.

"Did you find something?"

"That's the black Windbreaker guy. In this picture he

looks somewhat different than he did at the fire—he has shorter hair, and a mustache. But that's him."

"Are you sure?"

"Unless he has an identical twin, positive."

"Great. You're amazing!" He consulted a separate document he'd printed that matched each photo to a name. "Gregory Falen, twenty-eight. Two arrests for misdemeanor arson, no convictions. Does the name ring any bells?"

"The name doesn't sound familiar. But, you know, I can't get over the feeling I know him from somewhere. The memory is right there, hovering at the edge of my mind. The harder I try, though, the farther away it drifts."

"Maybe you need to let it go for a while. Let your subconscious work on it. Want to take a walk?"

Priscilla nodded, drained her coffee and slid her arms into the sleeves of a black leather blazer.

They headed out into Oak Lawn, which was very different from Oak Cliff. The two neighborhoods were among Dallas's oldest, but Oak Lawn was a mecca for wealthy young singles these days. On this particular evening it was relatively quiet, though the trendy restaurants were doing a good business. Roark and Priscilla walked along the sidewalk in front of the shops, quiet and lost in thought.

Roark tried to think of some innocuous subject that might distract Priscilla, but every conversational opening that came to mind sounded something like, *So explain to me again why you blew me off.* And he didn't think that would be helpful.

They paused in front of a trolley stop just as one of the antique cars pulled up. "You want to take a ride?" he asked. The service was free and it ran all the way from Oak Lawn to downtown Dallas.

"Sure. My feet are tired—I just walked all around Northpark Mall. Twice." She climbed on board and Roark followed. They found two hard wooden seats facing each other and sat down. Aside from a couple of teenagers making out in the back of the car, they were the only passengers. "It was a bonding outing for my mother and me."

"Did you tell her we broke up?" Roark asked.

"Actually, I told her the truth—that you were only pretending to be my boyfriend to put a halt to her matchmaking. She wasn't happy, but it cleared the air. I should have been more honest with her about my feelings a long time ago."

"So that's good."

"Mother thinks I'm insane for not trying to reel you in. She never went on about Cory like she does about you."

"Cory. Your old boyfriend?"

"I guess I never mentioned his name before."

Roark's blood boiled just thinking about the guy and what he'd done to Priscilla. "Are you still in love with him?" He hadn't meant to ask, but the question just fell out of his mouth.

She didn't seem to mind answering. "With Cory? No. He bruised my ego, but he turned out to be someone I didn't think he was."

"How so?"

"He just surprised me. He had attitudes, feelings I'd known nothing about."

"He kept secrets from you?"

"Not exactly. It's hard to explain. But how do you really know someone? How do you know how much of yourself to share?"

These were profound questions to throw at a man when he was sleep-deprived. "If I had all the answers, I'd probably still be married," Roark replied. He hadn't known Libby nearly as well as he'd thought he did when they'd walked down the aisle. They'd spun a lot of happily-ever-after dreams of a big family before the wedding. But two years later, when Roark was ready to start that family, Libby had balked. It wasn't a good time, she'd said. A year later it still wasn't a good time, and she'd finally admitted that she might want to wait a lot longer. She wasn't sure she wanted to be a mother. And things had gone downhill from there.

A stiff breeze blew in through the open window. Priscilla shivered and wrapped her arms around herself.

"Feels like a cold front is moving through. Do you want to go someplace warmer?" Roark asked.

"I'm fine."

Roark wondered what could be going through her head. Before long, she surprised him by speaking her thoughts aloud.

"My mother thinks I'm afraid to get involved because I don't want to be hurt again. And all the excuses I come up with—wanting to stay in control, feeling overwhelmed, wanting to focus on my job… She says that's just a smoke screen."

"And what do you think?"

She leaned back in her seat, nervously running her fingers through her hair. "Oh, she's wrong. She's dead wrong. I just don't want to give up control. When you hook up with someone, all at once you're not yourself anymore, you're half of a couple. You think you know the other person, and then suddenly they turn into someone different."

"That doesn't always happen," Roark countered.

"It's happened to both of us. You told me you found out

after you were married that your goals were polar opposites. And I thought Cory… Well, never mind him."

"I guess it's a risk you take," Roark said. "There are no guarantees."

"I'm not into risk."

"Oh, really? Is that why you jump up on the roofs of burning buildings?"

"I knew you were going to bring that up," she said with a laugh. "That's a different kind of risk. If you understand fire, you can try to predict what it will do. It follows the laws of physics. A guy, on the other hand, doesn't follow any rules—of physics, logic, thermodynamics, inertia, anything."

"Guys are easy. Give them food, sex and football on a regular basis and don't take away the remote control. Easy."

He got a smile out of her with that, but she didn't seem inclined to continue the debate.

Roark's needs were even simpler. He wanted Priscilla back. In his life and in his bed. But he sensed that now wasn't the time to push. He had to give her some time to figure out that she wanted him as much as he wanted her.

The trolley completed its circle and reached the stop across the street from Starbucks again. They thanked the driver and hopped out. Roark walked Priscilla to her car, hurrying a little despite his desire to prolong the moment, because the wind blowing out of the north had turned unpleasantly sharp.

He couldn't resist one last attempt to reach her, however. As she climbed behind the wheel of her Nissan, he held the door and leaned in. "I'm really not that complicated. What you see is what you get. Open book and all that. And your secrets, whatever they are, couldn't possibly be that bad. I consider it a personal challenge to figure you out."

She opened her mouth, ready to protest, but he didn't let her. He planted a quick but firm kiss on her lips. Then he straightened, closed the door, and set off on foot for home.

Priscilla turned the key and her car roared to life. She switched on the heater, but she was too shaken to drive right away. Why did he have to kiss her? Why did he have to put all kinds of images in her head?

Worst of all, why did he have to say all those things that had her thinking about possibilities? Could her mother be right? Was she letting Roark walk out of her life without a whimper of objection simply because she was afraid?

Every relationship was a risk, and yet people kept finding each other, fighting, splitting up, getting back together. If they didn't, the human race would be doomed.

She took some deep breaths and finally felt steady enough to drive. Pulling out of the parking lot and onto Oak Lawn, she intended to head home. Three blocks down the road, she spotted a familiar figure on the sidewalk, his broad shoulders hunched against the cold as he walked.

She pulled up beside Roark and ran the window down. "Hey, stranger, need a lift?"

Surprised, he stopped and turned, not sure how to reply.

"Get in, I'm blocking traffic," she said. "You should have told me you were on foot. I'd have given you a ride home."

He hesitated a moment longer, then climbed in. "Thanks. It was actually pleasant when I walked over a while ago. It's only a few blocks."

"I remember where you live." She'd been there three times, after all. As she turned down the familiar streets, memories floated through her mind, stealing away her resolve to be strong and sensible.

A car right by Roark's front door pulled away from the

curb as she approached his building. Priscilla zipped into the spot. "I can never find street parking in Oak Lawn. Is this one of those ten-minute spaces?" She craned her neck forward to read the parking sign.

"It's two-hour parking," Roark said, then casually added, "You want to come up?"

She knew she shouldn't. Way too much could happen in two hours.

A familiar sensation stole through her body. She could smell his soap and suddenly she could remember exactly how his hair felt when she touched it and how soft his Egyptian cotton sheets were. She could almost read his mind. *Take a chance, Pris. Or are you a coward?*

She switched off the ignition and opened the door.

Chapter Seven

Priscilla didn't utter a word as she and Roark calmly walked through the lobby to the elevator. He used his electronic key to enter his loft, then punched in the code to deactivate his security alarm.

And then they were in each other's arms, exchanging feverish kisses. Priscilla dropped her purse and leather jacket near the door. His jacket followed. She pulled out his shirt and ran her fingers over his skin, reveling in the feel of the hard muscles of his back. He had one hand on her bottom and the other in her hair.

And all the while his mouth worked against hers, demanding, coaxing, welcoming, invading. She warmed up in a hurry and within seconds was hot all the way from her scalp to her toes—and definitely a few places in between. She wanted her clothes off in the worst way; she wanted his off even more.

He put his arms around her as he'd done when they'd danced together. Now, as then, she followed his lead, letting him walk her backward across the hardwood in the huge living room and around a glass-block wall to the sleeping area, which was dominated by a king-size platform bed. The room was dark except for the city lights that shone through multiple windows.

Roark sat her down on the edge of the bed, unzipped her boots and pulled them off. Taking off shoes had never felt so sexy. Then he peeled off her cashmere sweater, revealing the lacy bra beneath.

"Oh…" Roark reverently touched an index finger to the thin satin strap of her bra. "This is nice."

"My panties match." She was a sucker for sexy lingerie. It made her feel desirable even when she was dressed in her shapeless uniform. Not that she wasn't already high up the desire scale at the moment. Just the way Roark looked at her made her feel like a siren.

Roark's eyes burned. He wasted no time getting rid of her slacks so he could check out the panties. But he didn't admire them for long. He dispensed with the silky scrap of fabric along with the rest of their clothes and then ripped back the covers and pulled Priscilla into bed.

The feel of his bare flesh against hers made her shiver with delight and anticipation.

"Still cold?"

"Uh-uh. Hot."

He kissed her again, more intensely this time, pinning her to the mattress and throwing a leg over her as if to keep her from escaping—though she wasn't going anywhere. He trailed kisses down her neck and throat, along her collarbone and finally onto her breasts, sucking on first one, then the other, until her nipples were so hard it was almost painful.

She wanted him inside her.

It was always like this for her, at least with him. She was impatient, almost crazy with the physical longing that pulled her whole body tight as piano wire.

It was all right, though; she knew what to do. She reached between their bodies and grasped his shaft.

"You're playing with fire," he murmured against her throat.

"It's what I do," she countered with a low laugh. "Are you going to object or are you going to make me very, very happy?"

"I think you know."

He rubbed circles on her abdomen, then moved lower, combing his fingers through her soft curls.

Then he grew very still.

"What?" She parted her legs slightly, wanting him to touch her there.

"I forgot something." He kissed her quickly. "Be right back."

"Excuse me?"

But he was up and out of the bed before her objection had been voiced.

She quickly realized what he was doing: he was off in search of condoms. She started to call him back, to tell him a condom wasn't necessary. But then he would want to know why. And she'd had enough serious, soul-baring discussion for one night.

Roark wanted to make their lovemaking last, to show Priscilla that they didn't have to burn out of control every time they hit the sheets. But it was impossible. One touch from Priscilla, and he was in a hurry even more than she was.

He couldn't really complain, though, could he? She was so beautiful, like the most perfectly crafted white-chocolate truffle. And rather than savor her with a series of careful tastes, he was about to devour her in one ravenous bite.

He rejoined her and placed the plastic packet on her

stomach. "I don't think you want me to forget that. Getting pregnant your first year in the department probably isn't on your list of career goals."

"No." But obviously she wasn't up for conversation, because she picked up the packet and handed it back to him. "You know I'm not good with these things."

"Too impatient." He kissed her again and reached between her legs, stroking her gently, then sliding a finger inside. She was wet and ready and she made a small whimper of protest when he broke contact to deal with the protection.

Then he was ready, and she welcomed him home with a deep sigh. "Oh, yes. This is good."

A little too good. Roark was so excited that he was afraid to move. But he focused on bringing Priscilla pleasure. And then he began to move, and she sighed with every stroke, thrusting her hips up to meet him. He closed his eyes, and for a few incredible, amazing moments he felt as if their bodies had merged, that they shared the same space—heads, arms and legs, but especially their hearts.

Then the explosion came, and he clasped her tightly and murmured her name over and over into her hair until the spasms subsided and his senses returned.

They were quiet for a while as their skin grew cool and their heart rates returned to something closer to normal. Once Roark's muscles started to work again, he nuzzled Priscilla's ear and stroked her cheek. "I am really happy you found a parking space."

"I'm just glad it's not ten-minute parking."

He held her close. "Seriously. It feels good to have you here in my place. Are you going to run away again?"

She had to think about it for a moment, which worried him. But in the end she answered, "Maybe not this time."

Something inside him uncoiled, and his muscles began to relax one by one. "Will you stay the night?" He felt more anxious about her answer than he wanted her to know. During their spring fling, she'd never once stayed the night.

"What about the two-hour parking?"

"They don't enforce it at night."

"I work tomorrow. I'll have to get up early."

"Me, too. I'll set the alarm." He had to get to work finding out more about Gregory Falen. But tomorrow was soon enough to think about that.

Priscilla snuggled up against Roark. "I'm not sleepy. I shouldn't have drunk that coffee so late."

"We can talk," he said.

"Only if we talk about dumb stuff. I'm not up for anything heavy."

"What kind of dumb stuff?"

"Like, what was your first car? And who was the first girl you ever kissed?"

"First car... I inherited my brother's old Volvo station wagon. Not exactly sexy, but reliable. First kiss was Mary Helen Finn. I was in seventh grade. She was an older woman...fourteen. Your turn."

"First car, 1994 Mercury Capri XR2 Turbo. White. Convertible." It had been waiting for her when she got home from the hospital. "I thought I was hot. I got a speeding ticket the first week. First kiss? I honestly don't remember his name. I was at church camp and we were playing Spin the Bottle."

"What about your first lover?" he couldn't resist asking. "Surely you remember *his* name."

She sighed. "It's such a cliché. Senior prom. Jay Da-Luca. Baddest of the bad boys. I only went with him because I knew it would make my parents crazy. And I never should have agreed to that hotel room. Or the frozen daiquiris."

"Priscilla, I'm shocked."

"Oh, come on. Didn't you try to get some girl into bed after your prom?"

"I never went to my senior prom."

"Really? Why not? And I won't believe you if you tell me you couldn't get a date."

"Half my school burned down the week before," he said. "So they canceled it."

"Oh. I'm sorry. Does this have anything to do with why you became an arson investigator?"

"Yeah, it has everything to do with it."

She found his hand in the darkness and squeezed it. "I'm sorry. And here I thought we weren't going to talk about anything heavy."

He shook off the guilt that pressed in on him whenever he recalled the fire. "I shouldn't have mentioned it. Let's see…where were we?"

"First lovers? I told you about mine. Your turn."

"Mary Helen Finn."

"The same girl? How old were you?" Priscilla sounded scandalized.

"I dated Mary Helen for four years. And I waited most of those four years, too. We finally slept together the night before she went off to college. I was seventeen." Still cocky. Still thought he would rule the world. That was a year before the fire at his school.

"And you didn't stay together?"

"No." He heaved an exaggerated sigh. "Sadly, she met someone else."

"Any lingering feelings?"

He laughed. "No. She was bossy as a drill sergeant, and she'd have made me become a doctor."

"I can't believe you dated the same girl for four years. I had at least ten boyfriends in high school. You must be…unusually loyal or something."

"I am," he said, completely serious. "If you let me into your life, I'm not going to suddenly drop out. I'm not going to stop calling. I'm not going to cheat.

"You're the first woman I've met in ten years who made me feel anything more than a passing interest. I see potential here. I'm not going to toss it away on a whim."

"*If* I let you into my life? I thought I just did."

"Unless you run again."

"No, not this time." For better or worse, she was going to give this relationship thing another try. Roark deserved her best effort. "It scares me, though—the whole 'losing control' thing."

"I can't guarantee things are going to work out. But if you're going to lose control, lose it with me. I'm a good bet. I'm solid. Just jump—I won't let you fall."

PRISCILLA AWOKE A FEW minutes before the alarm went off, propped herself up on one elbow and watched Roark sleep.

She was still thinking about the story he'd told her last night. Four years with his high school girlfriend—and she'd been bossy. That said something about his loyalty.

She couldn't remember everything else he'd said, but somehow, he had put her mind and her heart at ease. He wasn't going anywhere. She could trust him with her tricky, fragile feelings.

She'd had no idea that Roark took her—took their relationship—so seriously. Not until last night. Yeah, she'd known he wanted her. But the whole "potential" thing just blew her away. "Potential" meant he was thinking possible long-term. Possible serious.

Possible marriage?

Don't go borrowing trouble. She would take this one day at a time.

Unable to resist a touch, Priscilla woke Roark up and they made love again, slowly for a change, with few words exchanged. She'd wanted to lie there afterward, sheltered in his arms, but duty called. For the first time since she'd started working at Station 59, she wasn't looking forward to getting up and going to work.

AT SIX IN THE MORNING, Priscilla's house was dark and quiet. She put her key in the door and entered as silently as possible, hoping to elude detection. It was like when she was a teenager, coming home hours after her curfew.

No such luck. Tony was just on his way out the door in his jogging clothes, trying to be equally discreet. He pulled up short and stared at Priscilla, surprised, then slowly grinned. "Uh-*huh*."

"Not a word."

"Aw, Pris, come on. You come traipsing in at dawn wearing yesterday's clothes, and I can't say anything? You're asking too much."

She actually smiled. "Okay, never mind. That was just a knee-jerk reaction. Tease me all you want."

He drew back, suspicious. "Are you using reverse psychology on me?"

"Not at all. I have a boyfriend, I'm happy I have a boyfriend and nothing you can say will bother me."

Julie appeared at the doorway to their apartment, also wearing running clothes. "We're talking about Roark, I hope."

"Roark," Priscilla confirmed. She turned and headed up the stairs to her apartment, wishing she could just go back to bed and savor the past few hours in her head for a while.

Julie had the nerve to follow her. "You can't leave it like that. What happened? I thought he was just posing as a boyfriend to get your mother off your back."

"It did start that way." Priscilla turned and blocked both Julie and Tony from following her up the stairs. "Don't you two have some running to do?"

Obviously disappointed that Priscilla wasn't about to fill them in, they turned and descended, and she found refuge in her apartment. She actually would have liked to tell someone what was going on.

Julie would understand. She'd been through a nasty broken engagement and yet she'd been able to put aside her doubts and fears and marry Tony.

But Julie was married to a firefighter, and firefighters gossiped. Priscilla had fought long and hard to earn some respect at the station and she didn't want that respect disintegrating because her love life had turned into a soap opera.

Still, *Cosmopolitan* was a poor substitute for a living, breathing friend who would listen and offer advice and comfort. Funny how being in love could be the happiest and most difficult condition all at the same time.

Whoa. Love?

She wasn't in love. That was preposterous.

Chapter Eight

Priscilla refused to believe she was in love. Love was a long way off, and so was any obligation she had to provide Roark with highly personal information. He claimed to be an open book. But he hadn't told her everything, either. The fire at his high school, for example. What had happened to affect him so profoundly?

Would he tell her if she asked?

He probably would. Though she'd given him little reason to, he seemed to trust Priscilla. He appeared to have no reservations about them. But what exactly did she feel about him?

She pondered the possibilities as she scrubbed the floor of the apparatus room with cleanser and a long-handled push broom, the chore Captain Campeon had given her, Ethan and Tony because they'd been thirty seconds late that morning.

And because they were rookies and no one had tortured them lately.

Just because she couldn't go five minutes without thinking about Roark, that didn't mean she was in love. It seemed more like infatuation to her. She and Tony had talked about this subject at length, when he'd declared himself in love with Julie after the briefest of courtships. Before Julie, he'd "fallen in love" with one woman after another, when really he'd just been a mass of hormones.

In all her wisdom, she had convinced Tony he was not in love with Julie. But she'd been wrong.

Maybe she didn't understand love. With Cory the process had been slow, a gradual dawning. But maybe with the right person it *could* happen lightning quick.

Roark had seen her at her worst—with no makeup, hair in curlers—and he hadn't run for the hills. He'd endured her mother's fawning and her father's be-gentle-with-her-heart speech and he was still interested in her.

Was that love?

She realized she'd been scrubbing the same oil spot for five minutes. And now the spot was gone and she'd damn near scrubbed a hole in the concrete.

She was similarly distracted as she did the station laundry, nearly pouring bleach into a load of dark blue towels. This was one reason she'd resisted Roark: the uncertainty of knowing what came next and the lack of concentration that came with the territory.

Cesar Gonzales, who was the most junior man on the C shift except for the rookies, brought her an armload of towels. "Women's work," he grumbled. "That's all they think I'm good for."

Cesar had recently been denied the promotion he'd been hoping for. Priscilla let the chauvinistic comment pass as she took the towels from him. "You'll get it next time, Cesar."

"What would you know? You don't have a family to support. The department doesn't care about that, they just care about the bottom line." And he stalked away.

It had crossed Priscilla's mind more than once that Cesar came close to fitting the profile of the arsonist—late twenties, firefighter training, disgruntled. But she hadn't mentioned his name to Roark. She had nothing solid to report and she didn't think it was right to say anything based on a vague feeling. After all, everyone complained about his job now and then.

She didn't want the search for the arsonist to become a witch hunt and she was glad they had a more solid suspect to focus on. She fervently hoped the video would lead somewhere.

Ever since Roark had raised the suspicion that the arsonist might be a firefighter, there'd been a subtle but definite chill at the station.

As Priscilla washed some salad greens for lunch, her cell phone rang. She dropped everything, dried her hands and pulled the phone from her pocket. It was Roark, and a thrill coursed through her body.

How she hated feeling like a hormone-riddled teenager. "Hi," she said, sounding annoyingly breathless.

"Hello, Priscilla." Roark's voice was low and sexy.

"Do you have any news—about Gregory Falen, I mean?" She'd been hoping her mug shot ID would provide a useful lead.

Long pause. "No, I just called to say hi."

"Oh. Oh, okay. Hi."

"You sound like it's not okay."

"No, really, it is. It's just… You know, the surroundings."

"You don't want the guys to know about me."

"Well, it might be misconstrued. But really, it's okay." She didn't want him *not* to call her.

"Actually, I didn't call *just* to talk. I think we should try going on a normal date, one that doesn't involve champagne and formal attire. Or mug shots."

"Okay, when?"

"Tomorrow too soon?"

Ten minutes from now wouldn't be too soon. She was amazed all over again at how addictive Roark Epperson was. "Tomorrow will do fine."

"I'll pick you up at seven. How about dinner at Havana Nights?"

Havana Nights. The destination she'd suggested as their fictional first date. It was thoughtful of him to remember. "Sounds good." Spicy Cuban food, lively music, maybe some dancing... Ah, dancing with Roark. "See you then."

She hung up feeling a little dreamy and then realized she was being watched. Tony, Ethan and—God help her—Otis stood right in front of her, gaping as if she'd just phoned the chief and arranged a golf date.

"What?" She tried to look innocent.

"Who's the lucky guy?" Otis asked.

This was her own fault. She'd been so wrapped up in Roark, she hadn't bothered to slip away to somewhere more private for her conversation.

No way was she telling. "None of your business. But he's *very* lucky."

"Last night he was, anyway," Tony said, and she snapped him with a dish towel.

"Uh-oh, Prissy's getting violent," Otis said with a grin. "Time to scatter."

But with the usual perfect timing, the station alarm went off. Priscilla's love life was forgotten as they all sprang into action.

ROARK DIDN'T WANT TO wait until the following evening to see Priscilla. So he was glad when a legitimate reason to drop by the station fell into his lap. He'd been working with FBI profiler Kyra Cameron to see if he could glean any more information about the serial arsonist, and Dr. Cameron had mentioned an interesting possibility.

"You say this Priscilla Garner believes she knows the suspect?"

"She said she was positive she'd met him at some point. But she can't remember where or when, and the name didn't ring a bell." The name Gregory Falen was undoubtedly an alias. Roark and his team members had been trying to get a line on the guy, but his last known address was a laundromat and his name hadn't popped up anywhere else.

"Do you trust Priscilla?" Dr. Cameron asked. "You think she's serious or just blowing smoke?"

"No, I believe her." Priscilla wasn't the type to make a bid for attention by pretending to have knowledge pertaining to a crime.

"Have you thought of hypnotherapy? Sometimes a memory can be coaxed back to life under hypnosis. I'm a licensed hypnotherapist and I'd be willing to give it a try."

He couldn't imagine Priscilla agreeing to be hypnotized. That involved surrendering control. Then again, she'd said she would do anything to catch the arsonist. "Can we set up something for tomorrow?" he asked.

"I'm flying to Houston tomorrow morning to consult on a case. But I have a couple of hours this afternoon."

"Great. We'll have to meet with Priscilla at the station where she works, but that shouldn't be a problem." He called Station 59 and cleared it with Eric Campeon, but he wasn't going to warn Priscilla. He didn't want her worrying about it.

He was disappointed to see that the engine was gone when he and Dr. Cameron arrived. "What's the call?" he asked Jim Peterson, who was on watch duty. Roark casually looked over Jim's shoulder at the computer screen. He tensed every time he thought about Priscilla out on a call, possibly encountering an arson fire that included a deadly surprise. And he knew that if he and Priscilla were going to last long-term, he would have to get over worrying about her like this.

"Car fire. Third one this week. Woman saw smoke coming out of her vents, pulled over and called 911."

That didn't sound so bad.

Peterson rolled his shoulders. "Any breaks on the serial guy?"

Roark snagged a rolling chair and straddled it. "Don't I wish? I just need to talk to Priscilla." Not wanting to arouse too much curiosity, he'd left Dr. Cameron in the deserted TV room with a cup of coffee. "She's the only one who's seen our prime suspect face-to-face. She also thinks she might have met him somewhere."

"You have a prime suspect?"

Roark shrugged. "At this point he's our *only* suspect, and not much of one. I'm grasping at straws here."

"He's not one of us, is he?" Peterson asked, looking troubled.

"No. No one in the department has emerged as a suspect."

"Thank God for small favors."

The engine returned a few minutes later. Roark let Priscilla peel off her gear before he approached her.

"Ro— Captain Epperson."

Otis laughed. "Give it up, Prissy, everybody knows."

Roark resisted the urge to pull rank on Otis and tell him to cut Priscilla some slack. But apparently she could take care of herself. In fact, she didn't seem bothered. She just kicked Otis in the rear as he walked past.

"What are you doing here?" she asked, looking bewildered as they made their way back inside.

"Business. I have someone I want you to talk to." He gave her no other details until they were alone. Eric had given Roark the use of his office.

"Hypnosis?" Priscilla repeated after Roark and Dr. Cameron had explained what they wanted to do. "Does that really work?"

"In some cases it works véry well," Dr. Cameron said. She was an older woman, stocky and maternal in appearance, with a reassuring presence. "But it's not anything like what you see in the movies. You'll be aware and conscious the whole time. You'll just be deeply relaxed. And I promise not to make you squawk like a chicken."

Finally Priscilla agreed. Dr. Cameron settled Priscilla in Eric's chair—the most comfortable one in the room. She put headphones on Priscilla so that if alarms or sirens sounded they wouldn't startle her, then spoke to her through a microphone.

Roark had never seen anyone hypnotized before. It seemed too easy to be true. The psychologist talked to Priscilla in a soft, comforting voice, taking her through some relaxation exercises. Then she tested Priscilla by having her raise her arm off the chair and lower it again.

"I want you to think about the man you saw at the house fire, the one in the black hooded Windbreaker who stood all alone, watching the fire. The one we know as Gregory Falen. Do you see him?"

"Yes."

"Can you describe him to me?"

Priscilla then proceeded to describe the man, adding several details she'd left out before, including the fact that he wore a thin silver loop in his ear. Her voice was flat, emotionless, and she seemed calm and at ease.

"Have you met this man before?" Dr. Cameron asked.

"Yes."

"Describe when and where you first met him."

Priscilla replied without any hesitation or even any surprise. "I went to City Hall to pick up an application for the fire department and he was there for the same reason. He said he was a shoo-in because he'd already been through training."

Roark scribbled in his notebook. This was good.

"Please describe your encounter with this man," Dr. Cameron said.

And she did, right down to the clothes he was wearing and the exact words they'd exchanged during their brief conversation.

"Did he tell you his name?" Dr. Cameron asked.

"No, we didn't introduce ourselves."

The psychologist prodded Priscilla's memory from several different angles, but they got no further information. With a few brief words she brought Priscilla out of her trance, suggesting that she would feel relaxed and refreshed. Refreshed, maybe; relaxed, probably not. Priscilla didn't do well at relaxing.

She yawned and blinked a couple of times. "That's it?"

"That's it," Roark repeated. "You did great."

"But I didn't remember his name."

"You can't remember things you never knew," Dr. Cameron pointed out as she put away her gear.

"You've given me a valuable lead," Roark said. "He has firefighter training."

"Which fits exactly with the arsonist's profile, as does his age." Dr. Cameron shouldered her equipment and purse. "Look for someone who lives in Oak Cliff or South Dallas. He's definitely working in a comfort zone. Captain, I'll send you a copy of the tape." She took off without any further fuss, showing herself out.

"How are you going to find him, Roark?" Priscilla asked as she shook off the last vestiges of the hypnosis. She did look more relaxed than usual.

"I'm sure the department keeps all applications on file somewhere, even the ones that are rejected. I'll start going through them. Priscilla, you may have just blown the case wide-open."

Though Priscilla would have loved to have Roark linger—even if they just talked about arson—he seemed eager to get on with his job. "Let me know what you find out."

"I will."

"Roark, I didn't do anything funny when I was under, did I?" she asked. "I think I remember everything that was said." But what if she didn't?

"You mean that part where you asked if you could do a lap dance?"

She gasped, but then she realized he was razzing her. He gave her a quick kiss, and then she walked him to the door.

Priscilla was jazzed to think that she might actually have been of some use in Roark's investigation. Suddenly she was hungry and so she went to the fridge to get a cold drink and an apple. She didn't really want to stay there, because the only other person in sight was Bing, sitting at the table, reading the newspaper. But the captain took a dim view of food and drink outside of the kitchen. So she sat at the opposite end of the table and focused on the TV, which was always on. She hoped he would leave her in peace.

But, of course, he couldn't. He put down the paper and wandered over, sitting down uncomfortably close to her and punching her none too gently on the arm. "Way to go, Ice Princess," he said with exaggerated enthusiasm. Otis had given her the nickname Ice Princess at Brady's Tavern one night, and Bing continued to use it even when the others had stopped. "Way to suck up to the brass. Do you really know something about the arson case, or are you making things up to get a pat on the head?"

Priscilla didn't dignify the question with an answer. Roark had told her not to discuss the investigation with anyone. Instead she stood up, intending to simply throw away the rest of her apple and leave the kitchen. But somehow she knocked her canned drink right into Bing's lap. It was an accident, but that didn't mean she didn't enjoy it at least a bit.

He jumped up, sputtering and sending cola flying everywhere. "You did that on purpose."

She nodded toward the captain's office. "Captain Campeon is right in there if you want to make a complaint."

Bing stomped out of the kitchen, and Priscilla calmly cleaned up the spilled drink, humming to herself.

HAVANA NIGHTS TURNED out to be the perfect venue for a first official date. It was crowded and loud but not so loud that Priscilla and Roark couldn't talk—if they sat close to each other in their cozy booth. The food was wonderful, and after a glass of wine Priscilla was relaxed and talkative. She didn't appear to be the same woman who only days ago couldn't bear the tension or uncertainty of a new relationship.

They savored their food and sipped happily at the wine. And when Roark drove her home, Priscilla didn't hesitate to ask him up. The second the apartment door closed, Roark had her in his arms. He'd wanted to kiss her earlier—when he'd first arrived to pick her up, in fact. But he'd held back. Because he knew once they started kissing, they wouldn't stop.

And they didn't.

By the time they reached her bedroom, she already had her shirt unbuttoned. She might not be comfortable with the fact that she had no control in the bedroom, but he loved it. He loved the absolute abandon with which she gave herself to him.

Although he always had visions of them slowly undressing each other, it never seemed to happen that way. He wanted to worship her body as it deserved to be worshipped, but they were so hungry for each other each time they were together, and tonight was no exception. Clothes went flying, shoes got kicked under the bed and then they were lying down. This bed might be smaller than his, but it was wonderfully soft and it held *her* scent.

He could have lived here.

Her hands were all over him, and for a few moments he lay still, almost gasping for breath as she explored him, touching in places no woman had ever touched him before. He was hard as the trunk of a live oak tree.

And then he remembered something. "Oh, hell…"

"What? Did I do something wrong?"

"Oh, no, honey. I just… I forgot to bring protection."

"Oh."

"I take it that means you don't have anything here?"

She paused a long time before answering. "I'm protected. Don't worry."

His brow wrinkled. "Are you on the Pill?"

She pinched him on his arm. "You're worrying. Trust me, I'm protected."

Roark sighed. Thank heavens. He'd have stopped, put on his clothes and driven to the drugstore right then and there if he'd had to, but he was glad he didn't have to.

He'd just resumed kissing her when something penetrated the sensual fog of his brain, some noise that didn't belong in their bedroom. He paused and listened.

"It's your phone," she said, her voice full of dread, which meant she understood the implications as well as he did. Only one reason anyone would be calling him this time of night.

Chapter Nine

He couldn't believe this was happening to them again. And only an idiot would answer his phone when he was in bed with Priscilla. But Roark couldn't ignore it.

"I'm sorry—"

"No, go ahead. Answer it."

He kissed her on the forehead, stood up, found his pants and got to the phone just before it would have rolled into voice mail. "Epperson, and this better be damn good."

"Roark?"

"Joe?" He took it back. There were actually two reasons someone might call him in the middle of the night. "Is everything okay?"

"Yeah, I think so. I mean, yeah, they're great. Danni's in labor."

"Are you sure?" Roark asked.

"We're sure. Everything's going fine. But you said you wanted to know when it happened."

"I did say that."

"Can you come? I mean, I know you're really busy, but it would mean so much to have you here."

"Nothing could keep me away. I'll be on the first plane I can catch. Tell Danni I love her." He closed his phone and looked at Priscilla, who was hugging a pillow and watching him nervously.

"Who's Danni?"

He grinned. "Jealous?"

"There hasn't been another arson fire?"

"No, thank God. That was my little brother, Joe. Danni is his wife and she's having the baby. Now."

Priscilla relaxed. "That's great."

"At one time, we didn't expect Joe to live. The fact he's bringing another little Epperson into the world…" Roark had to stop because he couldn't put it into words how happy he was for Joe.

"It's neat that your family is so close even though you live far away. So you're going to fly to Boston?"

"I want to be there, even if it's only for a day."

She sighed. "You can use my computer to make the reservation."

"You are a really good sport. I'm going to make this up to you, I swear."

"I'll look forward to it."

Roark threw on his jeans, and a couple of minutes later they were in Priscilla's second bedroom in front of her computer. "The first flight is at 5:17 a.m. I can make that one."

"What about work?" Priscilla asked.

"It's a weekend. I occasionally get weekends off. Anyway, I've got my team busy trying to find Gregory Falen—which is probably an alias, by the way. I ferreted out seven fire department applications from the past three years where the applicant claimed to have had some firefighting training. My guys are tracking them down one by one, checking them against Falen's picture and verifying alibis. They'll keep me posted if anything turns up."

Priscilla chewed on her thumbnail. "That seems an awful lot of trouble to go to just on my ID of some bystander. What if he was just there to watch the fire?"

Roark shook his head. "He's got an arrest record for arson, though the charges eventually were dropped. Anyway, right now this is the only lead I have."

She stood behind him and rubbed his shoulders. "Poor Roark. I know you've been working like a dog on that case. I guess it's only fair you get some time off."

"Everybody deserves a break. Even rookies." He reached up and covered her hand with his. "So why don't you come with me?"

Priscilla laughed—until she realized he was serious. "You want me to come home with you to meet the family?" she asked, not quite believing him. She'd thrown on a lavender silk dressing gown and now she nervously wrapped it around her more tightly.

"It's not like that," he said. "But a little trip out of town would give us some time together. I don't get home all that often, and I would love to have you meet my family. I think you'll understand more about me if you see where I come from."

"But won't they get the wrong idea?"

"You mean like your mother did?"

"Touché." Priscilla laughed. "A quick trip to Boston is more tempting than you'll ever know. I've never been there. But unlike you, I have no vacation time. And I have to work on Sunday."

"You could trade shifts with somebody."

Priscilla was definitely tempted. "Maybe I could… Oh,

no, what am I saying? I can't go home with you. It would be too...too..."

"Serious?"

"Yeah. I mean, don't you think this is rushing things a bit?"

"You introduced me to your family. Your whole, extended family."

"That was different."

He pulled her into his lap. "What if we both promise not to read anything into it?" he said reasonably. "It's just a spur-of-the-moment weekend jaunt. Our schedules are crazy, it's hard to find time to spend together. So for a couple of days we forget work and school and relax."

"But what will your family think?"

"They're the most accepting people you'd ever want to meet. They'll be cool with it. And anyway, everyone will be focused on Joe and Danni." He hoped. He hadn't brought anyone home since Libby, and that was fourteen years ago. Hell, he'd just have to tell them what the deal was: he was crazy about Priscilla, but they were taking things slow.

She shook her head. "Roark, you make me absolutely batty. Okay, make the reservation. But if any of the brass objects to me taking Sunday off, I'm flying back tomorrow night."

He hugged her and nuzzled her neck. "Deal." Roark knew he was taking a chance submitting Priscilla to his boisterous, irrepressible family. They might very well jump to conclusions, even if Roark told them he and Priscilla weren't serious. Yet.

But he wanted Priscilla to see marriage and family the way he saw it. Seven siblings, seven strong marriages. Most or all of them would be there. And his parents. Married forty-five years, and still they looked at each other with real affection. Not that there hadn't been troubles. But their love had gotten them through everything.

He knew it was way too soon to entertain serious thoughts about Priscilla. But if she knew where he came from maybe she would see she had nothing to fear from him. Sure he was a driven arson investigator, but he was also a son, a brother and an uncle. Family meant something to him.

He understood unconditional love. And if there was one thing he wanted her to understand it was that nothing she could say or do would make him lose interest in her. He wasn't like that other guy, the one who'd been stupid enough to break up with her. Why would anyone want to lose a woman as smart, sexy and fun as Priscilla?

PRISCILLA COULD NOT believe she had agreed to go to Boston and meet Roark's family—and for the birth of a child, of all things.

But she'd been feeling all warm and fuzzy toward Roark and she'd been so charmed by his closeness to his brother and his excitement over a new niece or nephew that she'd lost her mind.

But only temporarily. Her last chance at salvation was the battalion chief, who would have to approve the schedule change. If he was anything like Captain Campeon, he would insist she return for her Sunday shift. Although Campeon had softened up considerably during the past few months, he was still pretty inflexible regarding the schedule. If you called in sick, you'd better be at death's door.

And that went double for rookies.

She and Roark hadn't slept, but they *had* made love.

They had their priorities. But rather than try to catch an hour of sleep, which would have been worse than none, they'd packed for the weekend—her things, then Roark's—and headed for the airport.

Priscilla had thought she would doze on the plane. At the fire station, she had developed the ability to get her shut-eye when she could, catching a nap under almost any conditions. But knowing the ordeal ahead of her, she'd been way too keyed up to sleep.

Roark hadn't slept, either. He was like a little kid. She'd never seen him like this before, and it was endearing. He loved his family a lot—that much was obvious. She wondered why he hadn't found a job closer to home after his divorce. But he loved his job, too, and clearly he felt a strong commitment to it.

They were at the Boston airport, waiting for one of Roark's siblings to pick them up. Glancing at her watch, Priscilla decided it would be a good time to request a schedule change. She dialed the number she'd programmed into her cell phone, then stepped slightly away from Roark.

When she reached Hal Gomez, the B shift battalion chief, she succinctly explained that she'd flown to Boston to meet her boyfriend's family. Mentioning Roark's name might have greased the wheels, but she still was leery of broadcasting her relationship with him.

"I can fly home tonight," she said. "It's really no problem. But if I could trade shifts with someone…"

"Say no more. You just solved a problem for me. We're a man short on Monday—Winston's going in for dental surgery."

"Captain Campeon won't mind?" She was pretty sure he would.

"I don't see why he would," Gomez said, sounding confused by her concern.

Maybe she was being overly cautious. She had never requested a schedule change nor taken a sick day since she'd started with the department.

"Well, okay, then," she said. "Thank you. I'll keep my phone on in case there's any problem."

Gomez laughed. "We'll see you on Monday."

She disconnected and found Roark watching her. "Everything okay?" he asked.

"Yeah." She tried to look cheerful. "The schedule change was no problem." She was stuck with him in Boston—with him and his whole family—until Sunday night.

Roark slid an arm around Priscilla. "You cold?"

"I'm fine." She had brought a cashmere coat, thinking it would probably be too warm, but now she was glad to have it. "I actually enjoy cold weather, and I don't get a chance to wear my winter coat very often."

"I'm glad you're not cold, but that's not what I meant. You seem a little…tense."

Was she that transparent? "Cory's parents didn't like me much."

"Why not?"

"I'm not sure, but I think they wouldn't have liked any woman who had her claws in their baby boy."

"Look, Priscilla, my family isn't like that. If anything, they'll probably like you too much. They'll tell you embarrassing things about my childhood. They'll want you to play poker with them. They'll draft you to help in the kitchen. They'll feed you until you're about to burst."

"All right, already. I will try not to be nervous. But not all of us can jump into a group of strangers and feel perfectly at ease. Like you did at Marisa's wedding. Just don't expect that."

"No one is expecting anything."

She was only slightly comforted.

A small blue SUV pulled up to the curb a few minutes later, and a tall string bean of a man jumped out, grinning ear to ear. He had ginger hair and freckles and blue eyes— he did not look one bit like Roark, except for the height. He ran around the car and nearly knocked Roark over with the force of his hug.

"Welcome home, little brother. It's been too long."

"It's been a busy year. Hey, Eddie, this is Priscilla Garner."

Eddie turned his cheerful gaze on Priscilla. "So this is the new woman in your life." He winked at Roark and gave him a thumbs-up. "Very nice." And then he surprised Priscilla by throwing his arms around her. "Any girlfriend of Roark's is a girlfriend of mine. No, wait, that came out wrong."

Priscilla smiled—she couldn't help it. "It's nice to meet you, Eddie."

Roark threw their two small suitcases in the back as Eddie opened the front passenger door. "Sit up front with me."

"Oh, no, let Roark sit up front. I'm sure you two have lots to catch up on." She opened the back door and dived in before Eddie could protest further. She had never liked being the center of attention.

She realized, only after she was in the back seat with the door closed, that she was not alone. A little boy, somewhere between one and two years old, was in his car seat next to her.

"Hi!" he shouted cheerfully.

Roark climbed into the passenger seat and immediately

turned toward the back. "Hey, Christopher. It's your uncle Roark. Remember me?"

"Unca Ro?" he said uncertainly.

"Right, Unca Ro." He turned to Priscilla. "That's what they all call me because none of them can say Roark. Wow, I can't believe how much he's grown! He was just starting to walk last time I saw him."

"Now we can't slow him down. He has two speeds— stop and ninety miles an hour. Doesn't use the stop much, though."

He was a darling little boy, wearing miniature bib overalls. He had red hair like his daddy. Priscilla liked children okay. She got along great with Tony's daughter, Jasmine, and Ethan's stepdaughter, Samantha.

But she hadn't had much experience with toddlers.

Little Christopher pointed one chubby finger at her. "Who dis?"

"That's your aunt Priscilla," Eddie said.

Christopher wrinkled his nose, which already had a few freckles across the bridge. "Aunt Pris…"

Priscilla sent Roark a panicky look. *Aunt* Priscilla? Just what had he told his family about her?

But Roark wasn't looking at her. Eddie had started recounting all the grisly details of their sister-in-law's labor, which was apparently ten hours along and going strong.

"Let's go home first," Roark said. "If it's not going to happen for a while, I'd just as soon get settled and grab something to eat before the maternity-ward vigil."

"Oh, I guess you didn't hear. Danni's having the baby at home."

"What?" Roark said.

"What?" Priscilla said even louder.

"Yeah, she's got a midwife and she's having the baby at Mom and Dad's."

"What if something goes wrong?" Roark asked. "This is insane!"

"I though the same thing," Eddie said calmly. "But Danni showed us all the research. For a low-risk pregnancy, she says home birth is just as safe as one at a hospital. And she thinks she and the baby will both be happier at home."

"What does Joe think?" Roark asked.

"Oh, he's all for it. He has no great love for hospitals. Anyway, there's a hospital four minutes away if Danni has any problems."

"If she was my wife, I wouldn't allow it," Roark said indignantly.

Eddie just laughed. "You're so Stone Age. Priscilla, don't listen to him. He's really very reasonable."

Priscilla pretended *not* to listen. She focused on Christopher, who was bouncing up and down in his throne of a car seat, banging a plastic hammer against the padded bar that protected him.

"You bang," he said, handing the hammer to Priscilla.

"Oh, okay. Thank you, that's very generous." She took the hammer and tapped tentatively. "Like that?"

"No!" He took the hammer away from her. "Like this." He pounded away with all the strength his small-boy muscles could produce.

Hmm, no testosterone there.

"Christopher," Eddie said, "be nice to your aunt Pris."

"Aunt Pris," he said with a laugh and then started hitting himself in the head with his hammer and laughing uproariously.

"Should he do that?" Priscilla asked with concern, but Eddie just laughed.

"He wouldn't do it if it hurt. You must not have kids."

"No." She wondered if her lack of baby savvy seemed odd. But once she'd accepted that she would never have any of her own, she'd kept her distance from them—not because she didn't like them but because she was afraid she would like them too much. Holding a baby or feeding one might make her own loss that much keener.

She had to admit Christopher was adorable, even if he was making a lot of noise.

"Aunt Pris, Aunt Pris, Aunt Pris!" Christopher shouted gleefully in time with his hammering.

Roark must have sensed Priscilla's dismay at her new title, because he reached between the front seats to the back and took her hand. "Don't worry. The grandkids in our family call every adult Aunt or Uncle, whether they're related or not."

"Oh." That made her feel only marginally more comfortable.

Since Roark and Eddie were ignoring Christopher's shouting and banging, she searched around for something to distract the child with. She spied a furry blue bunny, which looked well loved, and picked it up off the floor.

"Christopher, who's this?"

At first he refused to be distracted, but when she asked the question again and wiggled the toy, he suddenly stopped screaming. "Boo Bunny." He accepted the proffered rabbit and hugged it to him as if he hadn't seen it in years. Then he held the toy in two hands and very carefully, tenderly kissed it on the cheek. "Love Boo Bunny." Suddenly he held it out to her. "You love Boo Bunny."

"Okay." She took the toy, gave it a peck on the cheek and hugged it to her. "Love Boo Bunny."

Christopher held out his hands, obviously wanting his toy back. They repeated the ritual a couple of times, each time seeming to delight the child more.

Priscilla felt a wistfulness building up inside. This was exactly why she didn't go out of her way to interact with little ones. She didn't want to yearn for something she might not ever have. Even if she did marry someday, and she and her husband decided to adopt, there were no guarantees.

Finally Christopher pointed at her. "Aunt Pris?"

"Yes, that's right. I'm Aunt Pris." She tried to believe no one would think the moniker had any significance.

"Aunt Pris love Christopher."

"Uh…" It crossed her mind to say, *But, Christopher, we only just met.* Then she realized how ridiculous that was. The child just wanted love, the more the better, and he didn't care who he got it from. "Yes, Aunt Pris love Christopher." And she leaned over and gave him a quick peck on the cheek and a hug.

He smelled wonderful, like baby powder and laundry detergent and something else indefinable.

Christopher shrieked with delight. "Christopher love Aunt Pris."

"Absolutely," Priscilla said, her heart melting at being the recipient of this unsolicited, unconditional outpouring of love. The small child didn't know her from Eve, but he instinctively understood that human beings were meant to love each other without reserve.

She proffered her cheek, and he rewarded her with a sloppy kiss. Then he threw chubby arms around her head and hugged her with surprising strength.

"Whoa. Easy there, bruiser. You got a heck of a career ahead of you as a wrestler."

"Tightend for the Patriots," Eddie said. "We got it all worked out."

Priscilla hadn't realized she and Christopher had an audience. But Roark was looking over his shoulder at her, his eyes warm with amusement and what she interpreted as fondness.

It was only a few more minutes' drive to the Epperson home, where Roark and his huge family had been raised. The four-level brownstone oozed vintage charm—high ceilings, intricate moldings, the most beautiful Oriental rugs. Yet it exuded comfort, too. This was not a home where children would be afraid to run or play.

And they weren't. Children seemed to be everywhere—children from tiny babes in arms to toddlers, plus a few older ones.

Then there was Roark's mother, rushing down the stairs to greet him with a flurry of hugs and kisses. She was a small woman with salt-and-pepper hair pulled into a careless bun and a face wreathed with wrinkles—from a lifetime of laughing and worrying, no doubt.

"And who have we here?" she asked, turning to Priscilla.

"Mom, this is Priscilla Garner. She's, uh…we're dating."

"Roark, you didn't tell me you had a girlfriend." She turned to Priscilla and immediately enfolded her in a warm hug. It was obvious that Roark had honestly come by his affinity for touching and hugging. "Welcome to our home."

"Thanks for having me, Mrs. Epperson."

"Oh, please, call me Margie. And don't stand on ceremony about anything. It's a little crazier than usual around here."

A couple of the older children joined the fracas in the foyer, hugging Roark, and begging to be picked up. For some reason little Christopher gravitated to Priscilla, hugging her leg. She reached down to rub his stubby brush-cut hair.

Roark seemed to thrive amid all the chaos.

"Let me take your coats," Margie said. "Eddie, put Priscilla's bags in Deana's old room. Roark, you can fend for yourself."

"I hope we're not putting anyone out of their bed," Priscilla said. "We could stay at a hotel if—"

"Oh, nonsense. Anyway, most of this lot isn't staying the night. All but Roark live not too far."

Margie led everyone to the next level, which encompassed an ultramodern kitchen, dining room and living area.

Several siblings rushed Roark. More hugs, more introductions. The names went by in a blur, and Priscilla had no idea which ones were siblings and which were in-laws.

"Let's go up and see how Danni's doing," Roark said to Priscilla. "I want you to meet Joe, too."

"They're in our room," Margie said.

Priscilla demurred. "Danni doesn't even know me, Roark. I wouldn't want some stranger intruding at such a private time."

He looked as if he were going to try to convince her, but then he let it drop. "Get something to eat then. You didn't touch your breakfast."

"One thing we always have plenty of around here, and that's food." Margie dragged Priscilla to a kitchen table, where one of the sibs sat feeding a small baby. "We have all kinds of cold cuts and two pots of soup—potato and vegetable beef."

Priscilla stood up again. "I can make—"

"No, you're a guest, at least for a few more minutes. I'll fix your first meal, but after that you'll have to catch as catch can. We're like a pack of wild wolves."

Priscilla laughed and tried to relax. Though both she and Roark had grown up with plenty of money, their early years had obviously been very different.

"So how did you and Roark meet?" asked the woman with the baby. Priscilla thought her name was Deana—or maybe that was the baby's name.

"We met over a fire," Priscilla said. "Actually, I took a class from him at the firefighter training school last spring."

"You mean he's been keeping you a secret all this time?"

"We didn't start dating until much more recently. It's not that… What I mean is, we're not…" Damn. Roark was supposed to take care of these awkward moments.

"I know. You're not getting married or anything."

"Right." Priscilla took a bite of her ham sandwich. Though it wasn't exactly lunchtime, she was starving.

"That's what Mark and I said, too. But little Sunny here had different ideas."

Sunny. That was the baby's name. So her mom must be Deana. "Sometimes fate does step in, take the bit and run," Priscilla agreed. But at least she didn't have to worry about an unplanned pregnancy. "Sunny's a darling name. What a cutie." Priscilla gazed at the infant, who was dozing off in her high chair despite her mother's best efforts to interest her in some peaches.

"Thanks," the woman said with obvious maternal pride, taking the child out of the high chair. "It'll be fun for her to have a little cousin so close to her age. I hope it's a girl, but Joe and Danni have kept the sex a secret."

The baby sat on her mother's lap and stared at Priscilla with sleepy blue eyes.

"You want to hold her?" Deana asked.

Priscilla was surprised at how much she did. "Yeah, sure. I'm not very good at this, though." She took Sunny from Deana and settled the baby in her lap.

"Nothing to it," Deana said.

Wow. Sunny felt so cuddly—like a puppy, only better. Surely Priscilla had held a baby before. But if she had, she couldn't remember.

She could handle this. She could enjoy the experience and walk away. No sweat.

"I didn't used to be much of a baby person, either," Deana confessed. "Never thought I had the knack. But then I got pregnant and suddenly I couldn't get enough of Dr. Spock and Babies 'R' Us. It's the hormones, I think. So don't worry. You'll catch the fever when it happens to you."

Yeah. In another incarnation.

Priscilla tried to brush that dismal thought away as she watched Sunny stick a thumb in her mouth. But something curled in the vicinity of Priscilla's womb. Darn it, that wasn't supposed to happen.

She was almost relieved when Sunny started fussing and Deana took her back. She hadn't realized how strong those mothering instincts were—even in an infertile woman. First she'd gotten almost teary playing love-the-bunny with Christopher and now she wanted to snuggle an infant she hadn't laid eyes on until a few minutes ago.

She wasn't normally like this. She'd always made it a point *not* to turn to mush around babies. That sort of behavior was for girlie-girls. But she was tired and she'd let her guard down.

Funny, she hadn't even known she'd had her guard *up*.

Chapter Ten

Priscilla ate some of the vegetable-beef soup, which was delicious, and felt a bit more centered. She was okay now.

Roark reappeared, his face animated in a way Priscilla had never seen it. "Priscilla, Joe and Danni want to meet you."

"Are you sure?" Priscilla still felt like an intruder.

"I'm sure. Don't worry, Danni's handling the pain really well. She's totally cool."

Priscilla had seen women in labor. As part of her training, she'd worked a rotation in the Parkland Medical Center labor-and-delivery unit. If Danni had been in labor nine or ten hours, there was no way she was "totally cool." More likely Roark was simply in denial.

But he didn't give Priscilla much choice. He half dragged her up the ornate staircase, excited to get back to the action. But at the landing between the two floors he suddenly paused.

"I should warn you," he said. "My brother is in a wheelchair and he has some pretty bad scars. He was in a fire."

"The fire at your school?"

Roark nodded. "I'll tell you more about it later if you want to know."

Yes, she did want to know. And she realized now that she should have just asked him about it when he'd mentioned it the first time. He'd probably held back because he hadn't thought she wanted the gory details.

At the top of the stairs was a small sitting area with a couple of comfy-looking chairs and reading lamps. Several doors led to what Priscilla assumed were bedrooms. One door was ajar, and Roark headed for it. He took Priscilla's hand and in they went.

Priscilla took it all in quickly—the huge bedroom decorated in restful pastels and the three people, whom she assumed were father-to-be, mother-to-be and midwife.

Even Roark's warning hadn't prepared her for Joe Epperson. His face was so scarred that it was painful to see, his nose and ears misshapen, his lips drawn tight. But the bright blue eyes were alive with humor and intelligence, and the tight expression transformed into a welcoming smile.

"Priscilla," he said, stretching out his hand. "I'm so sorry."

"Sorry?" she said, puzzled, as she shook his hand.

"That you're stuck with my brother."

"Oh, Joe, stop it!" The admonition came from the woman lying on the bed, propped up on what looked like a few dozen pillows. With her short, baby-fine blond hair and elfin features, she looked like a pixie who'd swallowed a Volkswagen. "Hi, I'm Danni."

Priscilla took her hand and squeezed it. "I apologize for intruding," she said, even if Roark had insisted Danni was okay with Priscilla's presence. "Roark has this way of making everything sound so reasonable."

Joe laughed. "I can hear it now. 'Come for a relaxing weekend in Boston. Surrounded by my insane family and one screaming woman.'"

"I have not screamed once," Danni said. "Priscilla, this is my midwife, Nancy Wilkins."

The other woman, seated in a chair near the bed, wore yellow hospital scrubs festooned with teddy bears. She waved. "Hello."

"She's been reading to us from the tabloids," Danni said. "Anything to keep my mind off—yow!"

Joe grabbed one of his wife's hands, while the midwife monitored Danni's pulse.

"Breathe," Joe said, looking anxious.

"Squeeze Joe's hand," Nancy instructed calmly. "Breathe with the pain, that's good. You're doing fine."

Joe was also looking at his watch. When the contraction passed, he breathed a bigger sigh than Danni. "That one was longer, sweetie," he said. "And it was less than four minutes from the last one."

"Don't you think I know that?" Danni snapped at Joe, who looked like a kicked puppy. Then her face softened with contrition. "Oh, no, I'm so sorry. That just popped out. It hurts more than it did before."

"Let's check your dilation," Nancy said.

Priscilla and Roark made a quick exit.

Roark grinned. "Jeez, you're white as a sheet."

Priscilla didn't doubt it.

"Have you not seen a woman in labor before?" Roark asked, sounding concerned.

"Of course I've seen women in labor. I'm a firefighter." But this was so much more personal. "I just don't think we should intrude on Danni. I feel like a voyeur."

"I guess because we all grew up in each other's pockets, we're not very hung up about privacy."

"I live in a firehouse with a bunch of men. I'm not overly concerned with privacy."

He put his arms around her and hugged her. "Okay, maybe you're right. So what do you think of my family?"

"What a question. If I didn't like them, would I tell you?" She punched him lightly. "They're all really nice. But they're making assumptions about us. Not that I'm surprised. Bringing me here for such an important event implies we're, you know, serious. But weren't you going to say something to them?"

"I will. But I haven't brought a girl home to meet the family since Libby, so we can't really blame them for overreacting."

Holy cow. He was in college when he met Libby, he'd said. That had to be more than a dozen years ago. He hadn't brought a single girlfriend to meet his parents in all that time?

She wasn't going to think about that. It freaked her out. He had promised not to read anything into this trip, and she was going to take him at his word. If the family drew the wrong conclusions, she shouldn't worry about it.

"Want to take a nap?" Roark asked.

"No, I'm fine. But maybe we could find a quiet corner and sort of…decompress."

Roark grinned. "You'll get used to them."

The kitchen was deserted for once, and Roark and Priscilla loaded the dishwasher in companionable silence. But Priscilla remembered there was something she wanted to ask. "Do you want to tell me more about the fire at your school?"

Roark didn't answer for several long seconds. "Joe and I both went to a boarding school in Maine. I went there because I got a lacrosse scholarship—"

"You played lacrosse?"

"Used to. If you want to play lacrosse, Bremmer is the school to go to. Joe went there, too. Mostly because at that age he idolized me and wanted to do everything I did.

"Just before my graduation, a fire started in the boys' dormitory. A lot of kids were injured. No one died, but Joe almost did, and his injuries were by far the worst. I always felt like…like I should have saved him."

"Oh, Roark. I'm sure you did everything you could. Anyway, you were only a kid."

"I know. I've told myself that over and over. But it's still hard. It was an arson fire. A maintenance man who'd lost his job at the school confessed to it."

God. No wonder Roark had become interested in arson. And no wonder he was so driven to catch the arsonist who'd killed those firefighters. The arsonist who would undoubtedly kill more if they didn't find him soon.

"I'm sorry, Roark. Your brother seems like a great guy."

"He's never let his injuries stop him from living a full life. Never complained, though I know the pain must have been horrific. He went on to college and then law school. He's a prosecutor. I thank God every day for Danni. She saw past the scars to the person he is. We were all so happy when he got married two years ago. And then the baby… His life is complete now, and he deserves to be happy."

When they'd done all they could in the kitchen, they retreated to the den, where some of the adults were watching a movie. Roark and Priscilla settled on one end of a long leather sofa, and before five minutes had passed Priscilla was nodding off. She laid her head on Roark's shoulder and gave in to exhaustion.

The thought that was floating through her brain as she drifted off was troubling.

Did Roark equate babies with completion? With happiness?

ROARK STIRRED AND realized at once that he and Priscilla had both fallen asleep. Then he realized what had awakened him. His sister Deana was shaking his shoulder.

"Come on, sleepyheads. It's time."

On cue, a scream drifted down the stairs. Priscilla sat up and shot him a troubled look.

"It's okay," Deana said. "She's fine—I just checked. The midwife told her to scream as much as she felt like it, so she is."

"Is she having the baby right now?" Roark asked.

"Soon. Next few minutes."

Upstairs, they found a large crowd gathered in the small sitting area, including a few newcomers.

"About time you woke up," said Eddie. Roark greeted yet more siblings and made introductions. In all there were almost a dozen people there. In addition to Roark's family, Danni's mom and two sisters were there. It was like a hospital waiting room but with better decor and refreshments. Someone had set up a coffee pot and some snacks on a table against one wall.

At least there weren't any kids up here. Priscilla understood the desire to make the birth of a child a happy family occasion instead of isolating the mother in a sterile hospital environment. But she didn't think kids would benefit from hearing the screams.

Priscilla wasn't benefiting a lot herself. As much as

she wished she could get pregnant, she didn't mind skipping this part.

Everyone grew quiet as the midwife's voice rang out with, "Push, push, push!" The order was followed by a long pause. No one in the room moved or breathed.

Then it came—a tiny, thready baby's cry that rapidly grew more robust. Roark's mother burst into tears. Some people laughed with relief. A couple of people cheered and clapped.

"Boy or girl?" someone called out.

The door to the master bedroom opened a crack, and Joe's voice cried out, "Boy! It's a boy! I'm a dad!" Then the door closed again.

Suddenly Priscilla felt an unexpected lump in her own throat. She'd only exchanged half a dozen words with the parents, and the birth of this child shouldn't have had any particular emotional impact on her.

But she was touched and a little bit thrilled to be a part of this, no matter how small a part. Joe's unfettered joy had transformed his scarred face into a thing of beauty.

Priscilla's loss of fertility suddenly seemed fresh again. She'd thought she had come to terms with it. But she'd never before been this close to what she'd had to give up.

One of Roark's sisters—Kelly?—headed for the stairs. "I'll go down and let the little ones know." Others were dialing madly on their cell phones to alert friends and relatives who couldn't be there.

Priscilla looked over at Roark, who was standing off by himself. He had a hand covering his mouth, and his eyes had teared up.

Oh, God.

Her rough, tough arson investigator was about to cry over the birth of his nephew. And she just knew what he was thinking. She could almost read his mind. He wanted a child. He wanted this experience for himself. How could he not when every single one of his seven siblings had kids?

Her heart ached as the realization kicked in again, more emphatically this time. She could not give Roark the one experience he most wanted.

A few minutes later the bedroom door opened and Nancy, the midwife, wheeled out Joe's chair while Joe cradled his new child in his arms as if he were a butterfly.

He was so tiny. Only a little over six pounds, Nancy had told them a while ago. But he looked perfect in every way.

"Joe and Danni will be the most awesome parents," Roark whispered to Priscilla.

Probably no more awesome than Roark himself would be.

The room was hot, the heat turned way up for the sake of the newborn. Once they'd gotten a look at the baby, family members drifted downstairs to cooler climes, and Roark and Priscilla joined them.

"Want to get some fresh air?" Roark asked. He seemed to have recovered his equilibrium.

"Sounds good." She found her coat and stepped outside into the frigid air, which felt wonderful against her hot face. They sat on the front steps, each of them lost in thought.

Roark wanted children and wanted them badly. There was no doubt in Priscilla's mind.

It shouldn't matter. They *weren't* serious, as she continually reminded herself. They'd only started dating. If things got serious down the road, she would tell him about her situation and he could make the decision about whether he wanted to stay with her or move on to more fertile territory.

He wouldn't do that, her internal voice scolded. *He isn't like Cory.* Maybe he would be disappointed to rule out biological children, but surely he wouldn't be opposed to adoption.

After cultivating a few more reassuring thoughts along those lines, she felt calmer. She had no need to torture herself about this and she was determined to put it out of her mind for now. Though living for the moment was alien to her, she would simply enjoy the time she and Roark had together—however long that might be.

NOW THAT DANNI HAD given birth without a hitch, Roark could relax. He visited with his family and enjoyed the fact that Priscilla seemed to be getting along great with everyone.

"You guys serious?" his sister Deana asked later, when she and Roark were both bent over a jigsaw puzzle that some of the kids had started and then abandoned.

"She would say no." Roark found a piece that matched. "Ha, I finished the horse's head."

"And what do you say?"

He sighed. "I'm taking it one day at a time. But there's a chance. A good chance—"

He didn't finish the thought. A baby's cry caused Deana to freeze and listen. "Uh-oh, that's mine."

Roark stood. "I'll take care of her."

"She might have a dirty diaper," Deana warned him.

He shrugged. "I'll live. Who knows when I'll get to see her again?"

A few minutes later he found Priscilla puttering around the kitchen, cleaning things up. He was carrying baby Sunny, giving Deana a little break. "I wasn't kidding when I said my family would press you into dish duty, but you're allowed to say no."

"No one's asked me to do a thing." She gave him a reassuring smile and then tickled Sunny's foot, getting a smile out of her. "I like to keep busy, you know that."

"They named the baby Jeffrey. Jeffrey Austin Epperson."

"That's a very nice name."

"I'm on my way up to visit. You want to come?"

She hesitated only a fraction of a second. "Sure."

Did Priscilla like children? She'd been a good sport entertaining Christopher in the car and she'd known just what to do to quiet him down. She'd even taken a turn holding a fussy Sunny earlier in the day. But he definitely sensed some ambivalence.

Roark and Priscilla donned surgical masks and entered the bedroom to have their first private visit with the new addition to the Epperson clan. Roark strode right in, though Priscilla lingered at the door. He didn't hold the baby, but he got a closer look at him. He'd never seen one this close when it was only a few hours old.

"Don't you just want to run out and get you one of your own?" Joe quipped. Then he said in an aside to Danni, "He's always been so competitive."

"There's no way I'll ever outdo Jake," Roark said. Jake was his oldest brother, who had five kids. He'd adopted the first one because a doctor had told his wife, Marion, that she couldn't conceive. Surprise. Four times.

"No, but you'll probably have twins. Or triplets."

Roark cast a wary eye toward Priscilla, hoping all this talk about babies didn't make her nervous, but she had disappeared from the doorway. He knew she still felt a little funny intruding on the new parents.

"Take it easy with Priscilla around, okay?" Roark said softly as he closed the door. "She's very skittish."

"Hey," Joe said, "if she hasn't bolted yet, she's not going anywhere."

"She's crazy about you," Danni added. "I can tell just by the way she looks at you."

"I'm crazy about her. But her last relationship, she apparently got hurt. She's cautious. We're taking things slowly."

"Then why did you bring her home to meet the folks?" Danni asked. "That seems kind of serious."

"Spontaneous decision. Maybe not the right one," he admitted.

Joe shook his head. "If she doesn't like us, better to find out now."

"She likes everyone just fine." That wasn't an issue. But Roark couldn't shake the feeling that she was holding something back. Even when she was laughing, there was a solemnity about her, a wistfulness he couldn't explain in rational terms.

"Then what's the problem?" Joe asked.

"There isn't a problem. I just don't want her to feel like I'm pushing her to make a commitment."

"You think she's not the settling-down kind?" Joe asked. "I can't imagine you with someone who wasn't."

Roark couldn't answer that. He really didn't know. He'd been so determined to convince Priscilla they had a chance, so positive he was right about their chemistry and compatibility, maybe he'd been blind to an uncomfortable truth.

Maybe Priscilla wasn't a "forever" kind of girl.

Chapter Eleven

The Epperson house calmed down a bit after excitement over the birth subsided. People still came and went, but the air of frenzy diminished. Kids conked out or headed for their own homes.

Some of Roark's siblings wanted to go out for a kid-free dinner that night, and Roark and Priscilla went along. But he couldn't help noticing that she was more subdued than usual. Maybe it was just that she was tired.

They slept in separate rooms, but Roark sneaked into his sister's old room long enough to share a steamy good-night kiss with Priscilla. She didn't seem to hold anything back then, and he considered closing and locking the door. But there were just too many people around, and he didn't trust himself to keep quiet.

The next day, Saturday, it snowed all morning. They borrowed coats and hats and mittens—his parents had a closet full of winter wear in all sizes—and staged a giant neighborhoodwide snowball war in the park. Priscilla loosened up a lot, running and laughing when she got hit, crawling behind snow bunkers, shouting orders to her team. Some of the kids were surprised at what a good arm she had. But Roark knew she worked out like a demon and was as strong as many men.

By the end of the afternoon the snow was melting and everyone was exhausted and red-faced. Roark loved seeing Priscilla relaxed and having fun.

She offered to help prepare meals, explaining that she was trying to learn to cook so she could contribute to meals at the fire station. Roark's mother showed Priscilla how she made lentil soup and pot roast. Danni and baby Jeffrey continued to thrive, and Priscilla visited them several times and even held the newborn.

But on the way home the following day she went quiet. Really quiet.

Roark didn't want to return to their regular lives—to fires and arsonists and crazy schedules. If they could have stayed there in Boston, insulated in the cocoon of his family, he'd have done it in a second. Though he'd had to endure the occasional ribbing from siblings wanting to know when he was going to break down and contribute to the gene pool—he was the only Epperson of his generation who hadn't—all in all, he loved being with them. He still sometimes considered moving back to Boston. But, no, Priscilla wouldn't want to leave.

Whoa. He had to stop doing that. If she was hesitant about commitment, it might be because he was giving off white-picket-fence vibes.

It was late by the time they collected Roark's car at DFW Airport and headed home. Roark pulled up to the curb in front of Priscilla's house and cut the engine. He wanted to stay the night with her; he wanted her to ask him. But they both had to get up early in the morning, and he was afraid Priscilla was suffering from an Epperson overdose.

So he walked her to her door. "Thank you for going with me, Pris. It made the trip a lot more fun."

"Thank you for asking me. I had a good time. Your family is really great to make me feel so welcome."

"You fit right in. Everybody loved you."

"I loved them, too." Then she seemed to realize she'd said the word *love* and got very self-conscious. "Anyway, we'll talk tomorrow."

"Okay." He kissed her, almost turned away, then kissed her again as if he really meant it. "It was absolute torture sleeping in the room next to yours and not being able to touch you. We can fix that soon, huh?"

She nodded. "Sleep well." She gave his face one lingering caress, then went through the front door and closed it. Their good-night left Roark feeling reassured but unsatisfied.

PRISCILLA WENT THROUGH the next day's paramedic training in a daze. It was a day no one was looking forward to, the first time she and her fellow trainees would have to draw blood from real, live human beings.

Unfortunately the only humans available for amateur-hour bloodletting were the students themselves. Priscilla didn't mind getting stuck. She had a high pain threshold. But she didn't relish the thought of sticking a needle into someone else's veins.

At least her preoccupation with Roark and her own confusing reactions to all the babies she'd been around kept her from getting worked up about the whole needle thing.

Ethan grabbed her as his partner the moment their instructor announced it was time to actually draw blood. "Do you want to go first?" he asked, looking a little green. Poor guy. She knew he hated the idea that he might hurt someone.

"Sure." She followed the instructions about how to apply the tourniquet. *I can do this,* Priscilla lectured herself. If she wanted to keep her job, she darn well better learn how to do it. Several of the other students were expressing their discomfort in various ways, but she acted as if it was no big deal.

She hesitated just as she was about to insert the needle. "Are you ready?"

"C'mon, Pris, the suspense is killing me. Don't be a wuss."

Okay, that did it. She stuck the needle in. Ethan sucked in a breath but didn't complain.

"Sorry," she whispered. "Sorry, sorry." She released the tourniquet and was happy to see her syringe fill with blood. Then she removed the needle, placed a bandage over the tiny puncture and bent Ethan's arm.

"That was really pretty good, Pris," Ethan said, obviously surprised by her beginner's luck.

After giving the stickees ample time to recover from their experience, the partners switched places.

Ethan looked miserable. "I really don't want to do this, you know. Man, you have lousy veins."

"I'm afraid I do. Here, my left arm is better than my right. Let's give it a try." She'd received more than her share of needle sticks during her teenage hospital stay, and they'd ceased to bother her after that. "You won't hurt me."

"You're a brave woman." He followed the procedure just as Priscilla had. "Okay, I see a decent vein. Now hum a song."

"What?"

"Hum 'Yankee Doodle.' It'll distract you." To humor him, she started humming, and sure enough, she hardly felt the needle go in. Ethan was doing really well. He'd hit her vein first try.

But then something went terribly wrong. When he pulled out the needle, she started bleeding like a stuck pig. There was no pain, and Priscilla reassured a panicky Ethan she was fine as he applied pressure with his gloved hand to stop the flow of blood.

"Uh, Dr. Andrews?" he called to their instructor. That was just before he turned white and passed out. Priscilla caught him before his head hit the floor, managing to drip blood everywhere.

Ethan regained consciousness only a few seconds later, as most of the class bent over him.

"You okay?" Dr. Andrews asked.

Ethan sat up. "I'm fine, but what about Priscilla?"

"I'm okay." She'd folded her arm tightly against a wad of gauze to stop the bleeding and she was in the process of cleaning herself up. "It was just a little blood."

Dr. Andrews shook his head. "Every damn class, someone faints the day we do this."

"I swear, I am *not* squeamish," Ethan said. "Gimme an arm. I can do this."

"Not my arm," Priscilla objected. "Maybe you should give me a transfusion instead."

Dr. Andrews gave a hand to Ethan as he stood up. "You can try again next class."

Ethan didn't regain his normal color until he and Priscilla were out in the parking lot after class. They'd driven together to Parkland Medical Center.

As he opened the door to his SUV, he put a hand on her arm. "I am so sorry, Pris."

"Don't worry about it. I've bled like that before."

"When?" he asked skeptically.

"When I was in the hospital. The poor nurse drawing

my blood was ready to resign and join the Foreign Legion. You didn't do anything wrong that I could tell."

"Except pass out."

When they were both in the car and buckled up, Ethan asked, "When were you in the hospital?"

"I had surgery when I was sixteen." At his questioning look, she added, "Female stuff," which shut him up in a hurry.

"So are you gonna tell me more about your trip to Boston?" She'd given him only the barest of facts so far.

"It was…educational. I think you learn a lot about a man by seeing how he acts with his family."

"Uh-oh. Was it bad?"

"No, it was good, actually. Roark is…well, he's almost a different person when he's away from work. He's got this huge, boisterous family and a dozen nieces and nephews whom he dotes on. It snowed, and we had a big snowball fight and made snow angels."

"That sounds good, then. A guy who can get along with kids—that's a positive, right? Women like that."

"Yeah, it's good." If anything, seeing him with his family had strengthened her feelings for him. Unfortunately she'd also seen how wrong she was for him.

OF COURSE IT GOT BACK to the guys at the station that Priscilla had bled like a Freddy Kruger victim when she had her blood drawn and Ethan had fainted. Priscilla didn't know how they heard about the incident, but they had a field day with it.

They tortured her and Ethan mercilessly; even Tony, the disloyal bum, couldn't resist making a joke or two at his fellow rookies' expense. Since he already had paramedic certification and a couple of years of experience, he thought that gave him the right.

The only upside was that, with this fodder for the torture mill, they'd all forgotten about her absence during the previous C shift, so she didn't have to waffle about her "family emergency." Tony and Ethan knew where she'd been, but they weren't going to tell.

When Priscilla walked into the kitchen and found Bing Tate lying on the floor with ketchup all up and down his arm, she was about out of patience.

"Save me!" he said in his best falsetto.

"Are you kidding, Tate?" Otis said. "If your hair was on fire, she wouldn't spit on you."

"I would so," Priscilla retorted. "Of course I would spit on Bing. Maybe even twice. It would be my privilege."

The fire alarm prevented the vitriol from escalating. "All right, you two," said Murph, "call a truce. That's us."

Bing jumped up and quickly wiped off his arm with a towel. Priscilla dived into her turn-out pants and boots, which were stacked on the right side of the engine. She climbed into the jump seat, fastening Velcro and snaps as Ethan, Otis and Murph joined her. As they rolled out, they received more information. The fire was at an elementary school.

No one said anything, but she knew what everyone was thinking; all those children. Priscilla had never actually rescued anyone from a fire, but Tony had. That was how he'd met his wife, Kat—by dragging her and her daughter from a burning apartment building. His first ever fire, too.

She gave him a questioning look, and he knew exactly what was running through her mind. "You do whatever the situation calls for and you don't even think twice," he said quietly. "Don't worry."

She did worry, though. She was physically strong, for a woman, and she'd performed well during all the simulations at the academy. But a real rescue, with real lives at stake…children's lives…

As they drew closer to Wilma P. Hodges Elementary, the black smoke fanning into the sky led them right to the blaze. One of the "temporary classrooms," a mobile-structure among a sea of identical structures that had been built a dozen years earlier to accommodate the burgeoning student population, was fully involved—a big, rectangular Roman candle.

It looked as if every student in the school had been let out of class to watch the blaze. They were milling around, along with teachers who were trying to herd them away from danger. Impossible to tell who was in charge, who would know whether anyone was still inside.

If anyone was trapped, there was no chance. Every drop of oxygen had been sucked out of the air, and the internal temperature within that aluminum shell was far too high for an unprotected human to survive.

McCrae pulled the engine through a set of double-wide chain-link gates that someone had already opened. Another engine was right behind them—Priscilla could hear the siren as she jumped down from her perch. Two police cruisers arrived: thank God, someone to manage crowd control. All these kids running around scared her more than the actual fire did. They were getting close to the engine, curiosity overriding common sense.

With a singleness of purpose, Priscilla pulled the hose

from its rack, trying to hear the orders Murph was yelping above the noise of screaming grade-schoolers.

One hysterical voice rose above the others. "I can't find Connie Rivera!"

Priscilla closed her eyes for half a second, then opened them. She knew when she'd gotten into this business that she would face tragedy. But a child?

Captain Campeon arrived to take command. "Garner," he yelled after taking stock of the situation, "once we get it beaten back, I want you and Granger to go in first."

"Yes, sir."

Why, her? Why now? She already had her hands on the hose. But she surrendered the crosslay to Murph, got herself some tools, put on her breathing apparatus. She liked it better when *she* had the nozzle. Yet another one of her control-related characteristics. Fortunately she'd trained for this and had learned to deal with it. Sort of.

Ethan and Murphy McCrae used a combination of fog and straight stream to beat back a path for her and Otis. Otis went first through the narrow door of the temporary building. Inside, it was an oven. The spray was all around her, sizzling and turning to steam, and water was coming through the roof, courtesy of someone who didn't know enough not to dump on his own personnel.

"Connie!" Priscilla called. "Yell if you can hear us."

Nothing.

The classroom was a tangled mass of tipped-over desks, charred books and backpacks. Priscilla kicked debris aside, looking anywhere a small child could hide, but she found nothing. It was such a small space, she couldn't imagine how a teacher could have left a student behind. Unless she'd run out the door first in a blind panic.

"Does this thing have a bathroom?" Otis asked.

That was one way a child could have been forgotten. They found the door to the toilet and opened it. Ethan, who'd entered the building right behind Priscilla, pushed ahead with the hose, but the tiny room had been pretty thoroughly soaked courtesy of the water pouring in from above.

"There's no one in here," he said, and Priscilla breathed a huge sigh of relief. It appeared that Connie, wherever she was, hadn't perished.

The rest was routine—soaking everything down and trying to identify the cause. The source of ignition appeared to have been a small gas furnace, though of course one of the fire investigators would have to make an official determination.

As they were packing up, three preteen girls cautiously approached Priscilla. "You're a girl," one of them said.

"They do let women in the fire department these days."

"Is it scary?" another asked.

"It's only scary if you think someone might be trapped in the fire. We thought that might be true today, but fortunately we were wrong." Connie Rivera had turned up.

"Can I try on your hat?" the first girl asked.

"Sorry, but I'm pretty busy here—"

"Priscilla," Otis said, "public relations, remember?"

Oh, right. Just last week the captain had given them a speech about how they were ambassadors for the city and the department.

She moved away from the engine so her coworkers could do their jobs, and she took off her helmet. "It's heavy."

The apparent leader of the pack took the hat and almost dropped it. "Wow, it *is* heavy." She tried it on. Her whole head nearly disappeared inside. "How can you wear this without your neck breaking?"

"You have to have a strong neck," Priscilla said, helping the girl off with the hat and offering it to another. All three of them had to try it on, and then a couple of boys who had wandered up. She ended up giving an impromptu lecture on how they'd put out the fire, how the various tools worked, how they used the engine's various gauges and dials to regulate pressure. In the middle of it, she happened to notice Cpt. Campeon, watching her, arms folded, his gaze inscrutable.

Great. Now she'd probably get in trouble for shirking her duties.

A few minutes later, as she was climbing up to take her place on the engine, Campeon stopped her.

"You did really well with those kids."

She stepped down and turned to face him. "I did?" That surprised her. Although maybe her dealings with Jasmine and Samantha—Tony's and Ethan's girls—might have improved her kid skills, and she'd held her own with Roark's nieces and nephews, she still didn't think of herself as "good" with kids.

"I think I'll send you out the next time we're scheduled to visit the schools."

"Oh, no, not me," she protested. "I don't have much practice relating to children."

Tony overheard her and of course he couldn't let her comment pass. "What, are you trying to tell us you don't like kids? That's crazy. You're a woman. You got that nurturing gene."

"And you don't? Tell that to Jasmine."

"Well, it's different when they're your own. When you have your own kid, you'll see what I mean."

She should have had a half-dozen snarky replies on the

tip of her tongue, but all she could do was stand there, her brain frozen. Of course, he had no idea why his careless comment had left her speechless.

"Hey, Garner," Murph shouted at her. "Move it."

Everyone else was on board and waiting for her. She turned away from Tony, unable to settle on any retort, and climbed aboard. Ethan gave her a funny look, but she ignored him, too, and focused on pulling off her coat and stowing her air tanks.

They stopped at a fire hydrant to refill the water tanks. Tony used a special wrench to get the flow started, and when he did something wrong and ended up drenching Murph, Otis nearly ruptured himself laughing.

Priscilla managed to laugh, too. They'd needed something to break the tension. But as she showered a few minutes later, she wondered why she'd reacted so strongly to Tony's casual comment. Hadn't she come to terms with this baby thing years ago?

Why was the issue rearing its ugly head now?

If she thought about it for more than thirty seconds, the answer was obvious.

Having children with Cory had never crossed her mind, not until he'd brought it up so unexpectedly. He'd been heavy into his career as a lawyer and he'd often expressed pity for his brother, saddled with two little "rug rats" who sucked up every penny of disposable income and leisure time. That was why his sudden interest in having babies had so shocked her.

But Roark was a different matter.

So that was what had changed in her life. She'd met someone she actually wanted to have children with. It was no longer an abstract concept. And the fact that she couldn't conceive a child was suddenly painful in a way it had never been before.

She knew she was borrowing trouble and she told herself sternly to let it go. But wasn't it ironic that Priscilla Garner, the control freak who liked to plan everything and prepare for every contingency, had just run smack up against the one thing she had no control over—her own infertility.

Chapter Twelve

The alarm was quiet for a few hours, and for once Priscilla was glad. She wasn't at a hundred percent just now. She asked Captain Campeon if he wanted her to sweep the dead leaves off the back patio. He looked surprised, but agreed. She got a broom, put on a jacket and retreated to the back, where she could be alone with her thoughts. Sweeping leaves was something anyone could do, even someone as housework-impaired as she was.

Daisy, the fire station mascot, begged for attention from her chain-link run. Priscilla gave in and let the Dalmatian out to run a bit in the fenced yard. Not that Priscilla didn't have plenty of dog time at home. Tony had adopted one of the puppies Daisy had given birth to the previous spring, and the pup, Dino—now the size of a small horse—lived in the backyard they shared.

But Daisy didn't want to run. She wanted to play in the leaves, and every time Priscilla swept some into a pile, Daisy jumped into them.

"Daisy, this is not a game," Priscilla scolded, but the dog merely wagged her tail. Poor thing. Her original owner, John Simon, was one of the men who'd been lost in the warehouse fire.

Priscilla plopped down on the ground and let the dog jump on her and lick her face.

She wasn't normally weepy, but she definitely had a lump in her throat. "Well, damn." She had enough problems without all the guys in the station thinking she was a crybaby. She sucked it up, reminding herself she was supposed to be deliriously happy. She had Roark.

At least for now.

She heard the door and looked up to see Tony, a broom in his hand. "Need some help?"

She couldn't refuse, not when he looked so earnest. "Sure. Keep Daisy occupied."

"I can do that." He found Daisy's favorite tennis ball and got her interested in chasing it. Between throws, he helped Priscilla sweep and bag leaves.

They worked in companionable silence for a few minutes. Then Tony said, "Sorry if I said something wrong. I don't know when to shut up sometimes."

"What are you talking about?" she asked lightly.

"Back at the school. We were talking about kids and I said something wrong."

"No, you didn't," she insisted.

"Is something wrong between you and Roark?"

"Roark and I are fine."

"Okay. If you say so."

"No, really. We are."

He let that ride for all of about ten seconds. "Then why do you look like someone sucker-punched you?"

"I thought you were going to stay out of it," she snapped, then immediately regretted her tone. Saying something mean to Tony was about as bad as kicking

Daisy would be. He didn't have a mean bone in his body. He really did want to help.

"Okay," he said softly. "Really, I will this time."

"Oh, Tony."

"What? Did I do something else wrong?"

"No." She took the broom out of his hands and led him to the picnic table that had served them so well during many a summer barbecue.

"You hit a nerve, that's all. Roark's not the problem—it's me. I can't have children."

"Of course you can! The department has to give you maternity—oh." He cursed softly. "You mean you *can't?* Like, no chance?"

"Zero."

"Oh, man. I stuck my foot in it, didn't I?"

"You didn't know. It's not something I let drop in casual conversation. It's never bothered me much—okay, that's a lie. It bothered me a whole lot when I first found out. Then I got over it. At least I thought I had. But Roark..."

"Y'all are that serious?"

"No," she said hastily. "And I feel really stupid about the whole thing. We just started dating, and the fact I'm sterile isn't something a person normally blurts out on a first or second date. But I just get this feeling down the road..."

"You think it'll matter?"

She nodded. "He's a natural-born dad who just doesn't happen to have any biological children."

"That shouldn't matter. Not if he loves you."

There was that pesky L-word again. "We're not that serious."

"Then why are you obsessing?"

"I don't know!" But maybe she did. Maybe it *was* that serious. "Do I have to tell him? Right away, I mean?"

"No, of course not." Then he scratched his chin. "Well, maybe. Hell, you're asking the wrong person, Pris. I didn't tell Julie everything about Jasmine right away, and it almost became an issue. But it's hard to go blurting out all kinds of information when you're just getting started."

"Exactly. I mean, what if I told him and he thinks, 'Whoa, why does she think I need to know *that?*'"

"It's a tough call."

"I'm not telling him," she said stubbornly. "Unless it comes up."

THANKSGIVING. ROARK could have gotten the day off, but he decided to work. He couldn't go home to Boston for the holiday, not when he'd just been there. And since Priscilla was on duty by virtue of her lack of seniority, he decided to work, too.

Arsonists didn't take holidays.

Fortunately it was a slow day, though cold, wet and miserable. The previous evening, Roark had used his very Southern grandmother's recipe to bake two pecan pies. Priscilla had begged off, claiming she *had* to get some sleep before her Thanksgiving Day shift, and he'd let her. He'd kept her pretty busy the last couple of nights, he recalled with a guilty grin.

Lieutenant Patrick Wysocki poked his head into Roark's office. "Captain? I just got word. William Lancaster passed his lie-detector test with flying colors."

Roark sighed. He'd expected as much. In his gut he'd already known Bill Lancaster wasn't responsible for the warehouse arson—or any arson. He'd been the only one of the fire department applicants Roark had culled out of the crowd who couldn't come up with a rock-solid alibi for at least one of the serial arsonist's fires. He'd borne a vague resemblance to "Gregory Falen," so Roark had asked him to come in for questioning. But if Roark's BS meter was any good, Lancaster wasn't the guy. The lie-detector test only confirmed that.

So he was back to square one, hunting for Gregory Falen, who was a weak suspect to begin with.

As frustrating as his working life was, however, his personal life had taken a definite turn upward. Though he'd been worried he'd made a terrible mistake by taking Priscilla with him to Boston and thrusting her into his wild and crazy family, she seemed to have recovered from the trauma. Both their schedules were tight, but they managed to see each other at least every two or three days.

Priscilla no longer seemed as anxious around him. She relaxed more, laughed more. She even brought him around her parents occasionally. It was easy to see where she had gotten her control issues. He had never seen people as tightly wound as the elder Garners. But he also knew they loved Priscilla, and when they were driving her nuts with well-meant criticism and unsolicited advice, Roark had only to remind her of their love, and she immediately relaxed.

He looked at his watch and decided nothing was code red; he could slip away from his office for a while. If anything came up, he had a cell phone.

"I'm disappearing for a couple of hours," Roark told Wysocki.

The lieutenant grinned. "Going to see Priscilla?" Despite Roark and Priscilla's efforts to be circumspect, everyone knew they were seeing each other, so they'd given up trying to hide it.

"How d'you know where I'm going?"

"You've got that Priscilla look on your face."

He checked his reflection in the glass on his office door. "I have a Priscilla look?"

"Yeah. Kinda of a, well, a dopey look."

Roark wasn't surprised. When he thought about her, all the other junk in his life seemed to melt away. "Love will do that," he said before slipping out the door.

Love. Had he said that? It should have been scary as hell, but it wasn't. He'd known almost from the beginning that she was special, that she could be someone important in his life. He'd pushed thoughts of love and commitment out of his mind, though, because Priscilla had been so gun-shy. But now that he was reasonably sure he wasn't falling alone, the realization that he was in love, that he'd been there for some time, didn't bother him in the least.

He debated about when and how to tell Priscilla how he felt, but then he decided not to worry. When it felt right, he would know it.

For once, driving through downtown and south along the interstate was a pleasure, because traffic was so light. Roark made the trip to Station 59 in under ten minutes and was pleased to see through the windows of the apparatus room that all of the vehicles were present and accounted for, meaning no one was out on a call. He hoped the quiet would hold.

"Hey, Captain Epperson," Otis Granger greeted him when he let him in through the front door. Roark could already smell something wonderful, like turkey, dressing, corn. "What brings you out on this cold day? Oh, wait, never mind. Dumb question. You want to spend Thanksgiving with your lady."

"I come bearing gifts." He handed a box containing the two pies to Otis.

Otis lifted the lid and peeked inside. "Pecan pie? Where'd you get these?"

"I baked them with my own two hands."

"You gotta be kidding."

"Nope."

"I'm not sure I can eat a pecan pie cooked by a Yankee."

"It's my grandma Lily Lee's recipe. She was from Georgia."

"Well, I guess that's okay then."

Roark entered the huge dine-in kitchen, finding it an anthill of activity. Everybody said hi to Roark, including Priscilla, who was not exactly effusive in her greeting. But even if their relationship was common knowledge, they'd agreed to no public displays of affection on the job. Priscilla was still fighting to hold on to the respect she'd gained over the past few months.

"You're a brave man to return, Captain," said Bing Tate, "after the last time you ate with us."

Roark couldn't believe the jerk! Not only still ragging on Priscilla but calling attention to his previous bad behavior. Roark guessed that Tate actually thought he was a funny guy.

"Whatever's cooking smells good," Roark said, ignoring Tate.

Eric Campeon shook his hand warmly. "Glad to have another warm body at the table. We're short-staffed today, and it doesn't seem like Thanksgiving without a crowd."

Roark thought about what it would be like at his parents'

house right about now as his mom coordinated dinner for thirty or so. Little Christopher was old enough this year to really get into it. He probably had mashed potatoes all over his face.

Otis's girlfriend, Ruby, and Jim Peterson's wife and teenage daughter had come to the station to join in the festivities. Then Ethan's wife, Kat, and her daughter, Samantha, added to the bedlam.

Family was where you found it, Roark thought. For some guys, the fire service *was* their family.

Priscilla was busy mashing potatoes, enough for a pro football team, and Roark leaned up against the counter next to her. "You look perky."

"I am, as a matter of fact," she said cheerfully. "Since I sent you home early for a change. Oh, Mother wants us to come over tomorrow for 'festive leftovers.' She's inviting a couple dozen of her nearest and dearest, so if you want to skip it…"

"Of course I don't want to skip it."

"You really like my mother, don't you," she asked, sounding amazed.

"I do. Once you get past her tough veneer, she has a soft, squishy center. Kinda like someone else I know."

"Ha. My mother and I are nothing alike."

Roark laughed. "Two peas in a pod."

Priscilla paused in her energetic mashing, looking off into space. "I guess we are alike in some ways. I can't exactly deny that we both like to be in control. That caused a lot of heated battles when I was younger. She wanted me to be the perfect daughter with perfect clothes and perfect grades, and I wanted to rebel and wear ripped jeans to prove *I* was the one in control."

Roark laughed. "Face it—when you have kids someday, you'll want *them* to be perfect and you'll try to control their lives. You'll do it out of love, but you'll… Priscilla?"

The look on her face sent chills up his spine.

She handed him the potato masher. "Excuse me, can you finish this?" And she literally ran from the kitchen.

Either she was suddenly nauseous or he'd said something to upset her. He was betting on the latter.

Priscilla closed and locked the bathroom door. She didn't trust Roark not to barge in here after her. He definitely *would* seek her out. She hadn't in any way fooled him into thinking nothing was wrong, that she simply had a sudden call of nature. He was very perceptive where her feelings were concerned, uncannily so.

She'd been doing pretty well living in the moment, taking things day by day and not letting herself worry about where her relationship was going. Any time a worrying thought crept in, she would remind herself that they were taking things slowly and her only task was to enjoy herself. Roark had told her that very thing many times.

But how could she live in the moment when every person she met seemed determined to mention her mythical and impossible future children? It had started with Deana implying Priscilla's maternal hormones would strike when called for, then Tony and now Roark himself.

But what she'd seen in his eyes just now when he'd talked about her having kids—well, he might as well have broadcast it over a loudspeaker. He wanted a child and he wanted it with her.

She'd sensed for a while now that Roark's feelings for her were growing serious. The way he looked at her sometimes without saying anything, the casual references to the future, like when he suggested they should start thinking about where they would go when she got her first real vacation time.

As if it was a given they would be together next spring.

She'd brushed off any uneasiness she'd felt at times like that. Roark was just talking, just thinking ahead. He liked to make plans, as she did.

But she could no longer remain in denial. She had to tell Roark about her infertility and she had to tell him now, today, before he wasted one more minute of his life on someone who just couldn't give him something he had every reason to expect from a long-term relationship.

It might not be a deal breaker. He wasn't Cory. He might like the idea of adopting, helping out children who otherwise would be unwanted. But what if he didn't? What if he was bound and determined to have children the old-fashioned way? That had been Cory's desire, and though he'd made sympathetic noises about her condition, he'd admitted he wouldn't be happy having children any other way.

Some men were big on passing their genetics along to the next generation. She'd read somewhere that it was a survival-of-the-species instinct—and not at all uncommon.

She didn't think she could bear it if Roark rejected her. Cory's rejection had nearly killed her. She'd loved Cory, but her feelings for Roark ran so much deeper—deeper than love. He'd become part of the fabric of her being.

She had to pull herself together. She splashed cold water on her face and blotted it dry.

Someone knocked on the door. "Priscilla?"

Roark, of course. She pasted a smile on her face and opened the door. He looked so concerned it wrung her heart.

"You okay?"

"I'm fine. Really."

"Get your jacket. Let's go outside and get some fresh air."

"Oh, but they need me in the kitchen—"

"Ethan took over your potatoes. Come on, they won't miss you for a few minutes."

Why didn't the alarm ring and get her out of this? But the stupid alarm was perverse that way, always going off at the worst times and remaining silent when she needed to escape.

She wasn't ready for this conversation. But she had a feeling it was coming, whether she wanted it or not. She got her jacket and led the way to the backyard, grabbing a couple of dog biscuits on the way. Daisy was always good for a distraction.

She walked straight to the dog run and let Daisy out. The dog looked up at Priscilla with big, dark eyes, silently commiserating.

"Priscilla," Roark said, "I don't know how to say this except to just come out and say it. I know something about our conversation just now upset you. I also know there's something you haven't been telling me, something you're holding back. If we're to make any kind of go at this relationship thing, you need to be honest with me. And you need to do it now."

Chapter Thirteen

Roark led her over to the picnic table and practically forced her to sit, then sat down beside her.

"Does this have something to do with having kids?" he asked.

She nodded, knowing what she had to tell him but somehow unable to choke out the right words.

"I love kids," he said. "I'm sure you've figured that out by now."

"Yeah."

"I always wanted to have a big family. I want my kids to have what I had growing up. But just because I mention them now and then doesn't mean I'd pressure you to hurry up and give 'em to me. I know motherhood wouldn't be ideal this early in your career. But there's plenty of time for kids. So if you don't want to even think about children until your thirties, I'm okay with that. Don't let my comments scare you off."

Was he kidding? Was she supposed to feel comforted? Because everything he'd just said terrified her. She'd just realized something that was even worse than the idea of Roark rejecting her because she couldn't have kids. What if he *didn't* reject her? What if he stayed with her, stuck by her, pretended it didn't matter to him when it did?

If he could be a father *tomorrow,* it wouldn't be soon enough for him. Yet he'd just granted her a huge concession by claiming he was willing to wait for years. What other concessions would he be willing to grant? And at what cost to his own dreams?

He wouldn't reject her because of infertility. She knew it as well as she knew her own name. He was loyal and kind and compassionate. He would put her first. And maybe it would be okay. Maybe he would tell himself it was okay, they could adopt.

But what if they couldn't? There were no guarantees when it came to adoption or any of the cutting-edge methods infertile couples used to start a family. He would be devastated if they couldn't have kids.

He would regret it. And she couldn't bear to watch him grow bitter, to regret the decision he'd made to stay with her.

"What are you thinking?" he asked.

"I'm thinking that…I may not want to have kids," she said cautiously. It wasn't the truth. She did want kids. Maybe she'd been fooling herself into thinking she'd be fine without them, but being around all those children in Boston had brought the truth home.

She'd said what she said for Roark's sake. Because if he knew about her infertility, he wouldn't break up with her, as Cory had. He would stick with her because he was an honorable man. But if he thought not having children was her *choice,* he might see it as a sign of incompatibility, and leaving her would be easier.

When Roark didn't react right away, she filled the conversational gap. "It's probably too soon for us to even be talking about this, but since you brought it up and you've been so clear about your feelings, I should probably let you know mine. I might not want to have children."

"Ever?" His voice cracked. He looked like a little boy who'd just learned Santa Claus was really his dad in a red suit.

"M-maybe not ever." She couldn't have felt any worse if she'd kicked him in the teeth.

"You're young still. You're focused on your job, and I understand that. It's very demanding. But life will settle down."

"But what if I'm just not maternal?"

"Deana wasn't maternal. But she changed once she got pregnant."

"I wouldn't count on this to change, Roark."

He didn't say anything. He just stared at her, uncomprehending. It was on the tip of her tongue to tell him the truth, but she couldn't find the words. She couldn't bear for him to pity her.

"I would understand," she said carefully, "if you wanted to move on to greener pastures."

"What? What are you talking about? We've got a good thing going."

"Yes, we do," she agreed quickly. "But I know you want kids. And if I'm not the one to give them to you…"

He sighed and pinched the bridge of his nose. "We don't have to make any decisions right now. Later we can talk about it some more, okay?"

She nodded. At least he hadn't run away screaming. So maybe having biological children wouldn't be a deal breaker for Roark, as it had been for Cory. But she had a feeling "talk about it some more" meant he would try to change her mind.

Somehow they got through dinner. Priscilla felt a tightness in her throat when Otis, serious for once, said the blessing and expressed his gratitude for all the good things they had in their lives—their health, their families, plenty of food and each other. As the meal progressed, she participated in the banter, as did Roark, though he seemed a bit subdued.

Just as they were cutting into Roark's pie, he got a call. Everyone grew silent and watched as Roark spoke a few words into the phone, then hung up.

"Is it our boy?" Captain Campeon asked. Everyone had been a little jumpy lately. The serial arsonist had been on a pretty consistent timetable, a fire every few weeks. It had been three weeks since the last one; he could strike anytime.

"No. Suspicious fire at a shoe store but none of the serial guy's signatures." He thanked everyone for sharing Thanksgiving with him, said a quick goodbye to Priscilla and then left.

She knew this wasn't the last they would talk about children. He would bring it up again—probably tomorrow after they went to her parents' house.

If he didn't soften his stance, she knew what she had to do.

THE GARNERS' "FESTIVE Leftover" party was in full swing by the time Roark and Priscilla arrived. People were coming and going, some sitting down to eat a full meal, others picking at tidbits on cocktail plates and still others gathering in the den with TV trays to watch football.

Roark recognized some of the guests from Marisa's wedding. Unlike that event, however, he felt more at ease here. He'd passed some secret test among Priscilla's relatives; instead of singling him out for attention, they simply accepted him now.

"Here, Roark," Lorraine Garner said, passing a fancy corkscrew and a bottle of wine to him as a group gathered around the enormous dining room table. "This corkscrew requires training in nuclear physics."

"I managed to avoid physics in college," he said. "But I'll give it a try." After a couple of false starts, he got the bottle of Bordeaux open.

Roark had been doing a lot of thinking over the past twenty-four hours. The first thing he had to sort out was the question, could he be happy without children?

Satisfied, maybe. Content. But happy? A future with Priscilla surely wouldn't be a bad thing, with or without kids. But giving up his prospective role as a father would be tough.

The second question he had to answer for himself was, could he love Priscilla, could he commit to her for the rest of his life, if she really, truly did not *want* children? If she didn't *like* them?

He'd recognized that she wasn't entirely comfortable around babies and toddlers. But she'd admitted she hadn't had much practice with little ones. And she seemed to get on pretty well with older children.

If she just truly did not like babies and everything that went with them, however… That was troubling to him.

At least she was being honest. He suspected Libby hadn't ever wanted kids but had gone along with him to keep the peace, figuring they could sort it out later.

He'd always pictured himself someday with a woman who shared his love of children. And yet the only two women he'd ever fallen in love with were both ambivalent about them. Was it her age? Priscilla was twenty-six, the same age Libby had been when they divorced. Would she change her mind later? Libby had. He'd heard through the grapevine that she and her second husband now had a four-year-old son. Did he want to take a chance that Priscilla would feel differently as she matured? The fact that she didn't want to share the bond of parenthood with him bothered him—a whole lot.

What else didn't he know about her? What else hadn't she revealed? Not that he faulted her. She had, after all, revealed her feelings on the subject as soon as she realized it might be an issue. But still, it had shocked him. He thought he knew her—knew her well enough to fall in love, at any rate.

I wouldn't count on this to change, Roark.

Her words kept repeating themselves inside his head. But that was exactly what he was doing. He was counting on things to change. He wouldn't let Priscilla just drift off as he had Libby, only to have her fall in love with some other guy and build a family with *him.*

Marisa and her new husband, still sporting tans from their two weeks in Bermuda, sat across from Priscilla and Roark. They were so wrapped up in each other that they hardly noticed anyone else.

"Marisa, hon, you've got to try this deviled egg," her husband, Peter, said, offering her a bite on a fork.

Marisa took a bite and made a face of ecstasy. "Mmm, oh, my. Aunt Lorraine, can I have the recipe?"

"Certainly, dear," Lorraine said, looking pleased. She did enjoy receiving compliments on her cooking.

"So Marisa," Peter said in a voice loud enough to garner everyone's attention, "is now a good time?"

Marisa beamed. "I think so. Mom, Dad, everyone, we have an announcement to make." She paused, making sure every eye was on her. "We're pregnant!"

The table erupted in congratulations, with everyone jumping up to hug the new mother-to-be and slap the father-to-be on the back. With two notable exceptions.

Neither Priscilla nor her mother moved. Their gazes were locked, and they were communicating on some mysterious mother-daughter wavelength that left Roark clueless.

Finally Lorraine stood. "Well, this calls for something special. And I have just the thing. Priscilla, would you help me in the kitchen, please?"

Priscilla followed her mother into the kitchen in a daze. She hadn't seen that one coming. Marisa, pregnant? And beaming about it like a lighthouse? Marisa had once told Priscilla she would never wreck her figure—so perfect thanks to Pilates and the South Beach Diet—by getting pregnant.

But she *had* been the one to play with dolls.

"Oh, Priscilla, honey, I'm so sorry," her mother said the minute they were alone in the kitchen.

"Sorry about what?" Priscilla thought she could brazen her way through this, but she was wrong.

"Your cousin announcing she's pregnant, and in such a public way."

"It doesn't bother me," Priscilla insisted, looking around for that special-occasion dish her mother had mentioned. "What did you need help with?"

"I don't know, I have to come up with it. We had so many desserts from yesterday I didn't think it was necessary to make anything new." She looked in the freezer and grabbed two cartons of ice cream and a frozen graham-cracker crust. She stuck the crust in her convection oven. "And you aren't fooling me—I know it does bother you. When Marisa made her announcement, you looked like someone had just stuck you with a fork. And don't think Roark didn't notice. He notices every single thing about you."

Priscilla felt her lower lip tremble. Stupid lip.

Her mother, never a very demonstrative person, put her arms around Priscilla. "Oh, honey."

"I thought I got over this a long time ago," Priscilla said. "Maybe you should get your money back from that expensive therapist you sent me to."

"Because you're in love."

"You really think that's it?" Priscilla pulled away. "I didn't feel this way when Cory broke up with me. I mean, I was angry that he didn't love me enough to overlook my infertility and I felt about this big." She held her thumb and index finger a millimeter apart. "The breakup took the wind out of my sails. I had to rethink my whole future. But it wasn't because I couldn't have kids. Now it's different."

"No one said you can't have children," Lorraine said. She pulled the crust out of the oven and started spooning vanilla ice cream into it. Then she took a leftover pumpkin pie, scooped out the filling and layered it on top of the ice cream.

Priscilla wrinkled her nose. "Oh, Mother, are you sure?"

"Trust me." Over the pumpkin she sprinkled a layer of toasted pecans she just happened to have on hand, then another layer of ice cream.

"I know there are other ways to have children," Priscilla said. "But I'm not sure Roark will want to do it that way. You know how men are. They want to pass on their genes."

Lorraine stopped working on the pie and took Priscilla by the shoulders. "Honey, listen. That man loves you. I see it in his eyes every time he looks at you. He is not like Cory. He will accept you as you are."

"I know that," Priscilla said. "But will he be happy? I'm not so sure. And I don't want to bind him to me if he's not going to be happy."

"Then talk to him. You love him, too, don't you?"

"Yes," Priscilla said miserably.

"Then work on it. No one said love was easy. Now before you go back in, powder your nose and brush your hair. I wish you would take just a little more pride in your appearance."

Now that was the mother she was used to. "Yes, ma'am. But, Mother, I just have to say one more thing."

"What, dear?"

"Did Marisa get pregnant on her wedding night or what? It hasn't even been a month! What a fertile Myrtle!"

"Priscilla, don't be tacky." But Lorraine was trying and failing to disguise a smirk as she exited the kitchen holding an ice cream pie that looked as if she'd slaved over it for hours.

ROARK WAS SURPRISED when Lorraine came out of the kitchen without his girlfriend. "What happened to Priscilla?" he asked Lorraine after everyone had oohed and aahed over the pie.

"Oh, she went upstairs to freshen up."

Hmm. Priscilla wasn't a "freshen up" kind of girl. Her reaction to her cousin's announcement had been strange. And when he got her alone, he was going to find out why.

She returned a few minutes later looking and acting fine. They shared a piece of pie—they were both so full they could only eat a couple of bites each, but it was spectacular.

"Did she show you how to make this?" Roark asked. Priscilla had been learning how to fix all kinds of new dishes.

"Well, it's kind of complex, but I might be able to pull it off, since I've become such an expert in the kitchen," she said with tongue firmly in cheek.

"You want to go for a walk?" He needed to get her alone.

"Yeah, okay. It is kind of stuffy in here." They got their jackets and headed out the front door. It was cold and damp but not windy, and after a block of brisk walking they both started to warm up.

They walked in silence to the end of Armstrong Parkway, where workers using tall ladders and a cherry picker were hanging holiday lights in a huge live oak tree. It was tradition; when the crew turned on the lights tonight, cars by the hundreds would turn up to see the spectacle.

They sat on a stone bench in the center of the parkway median and watched a flock of starlings circle overhead.

"It's a deal breaker for you, isn't it?" Priscilla said abruptly.

"What?"

"Having kids."

"Priscilla, I…" He just didn't know how to respond. "Would it make a difference if I told you I love you? In my mind, creating a child together is the ultimate expression of that love. I can't lie. I want to see you carrying my child. I want to rub your feet at night and run out to the store at three in the morning because you want hot wings. I want to be in the delivery room, listening to you curse the day I was born. And I want to be a big part of my child's life.

"I wouldn't leave you to do it alone. I wouldn't expect you to give up your career. We could work out our schedules and we could hire help if we needed to.

"But is it a deal breaker? You mean, do I want to break up because you don't feel the same way about kids?"

He paused, wanting to be very sure he answered truthfully. "No. I still love you. I can't change that."

His words obviously weren't reassuring her. She pulled her legs up and wrapped her arms around them, resting her forehead against her knees.

"I love you, too," she said.

He'd imagined hearing those words but never under such trying circumstances. He lightly touched her hair, tucking a strand behind her ear. "Then there's no problem."

"Yes, there is. Love does not solve everything. We want different things out of life. And I just can't see you tying yourself to me when I can't give you something that's obviously important to you."

"Shouldn't I be the one to worry about that?" Roark said.

"No. Because I'm the one who would feel guilty every time I saw you smiling at someone else's baby or playing with one of your nieces or nephews. You deserve to have children, Roark. You need to be a father. You need to have those experiences—watching your wife grow big with your baby…getting cursed at in the delivery room…2:00 a.m. feedings. And I'm afraid that's not what you'll get with me."

"So you think we should give up?"

"Don't you?"

He honestly didn't know. He was in shock. He'd always seen himself with children—always. But he loved Priscilla. The fact she had some doubts about motherhood didn't make him love her any less, but it did make him wonder about their long-term prospects. She had a right to decide whether she wanted children, and he certainly didn't want to pressure her into it.

But a life without his own children…ever? "What about

family vacations to the Grand Canyon?" he asked in a last-ditch effort to get her to admit she might change her mind. "What about soccer games and ballet recitals? The first date? Senior prom? Wouldn't you miss those?"

She looked down, then away. She wouldn't answer.

"We don't have to decide now," he said. In truth, he needed some time to let this sink in. "These are important decisions we're talking about here. There's no reason to rush."

"Then let's just think about it," she said. "Maybe we should take a few days. A couple of weeks even. Then we can talk again."

"That sounds reasonable." Actually, it sounded awful. It sounded like something people say when they're breaking up.

Chapter Fourteen

It had been five days since Roark had last seen Priscilla, standing forlornly on the sidewalk in front of her parents' house. He hadn't even gone back inside to thank the Garners for their hospitality. But he'd been in no mood for polite formalities.

He had offered to take Priscilla home, since he'd brought her, but she'd told him she'd get a ride to the train station later.

And so he'd fled.

He had immersed himself in work for several days, stepping up his search for the serial arsonist. He had followed up every lead he had, even the ones he'd previously dismissed as products of the lunatic fringe, spending hours on the phone and knocking on doors. Anything to distract himself from thoughts of Priscilla.

But on the fifth day, after what had seemed like a hundred leads that went nowhere, he finally acknowledged his misery. He figured he wasn't going to get past it unless he wallowed in it. And what better place to wallow than Brady's, his old pre-Priscilla hangout?

He checked his watch. Damn, it was almost midnight. No wonder he was so hungry.

Brady's had the double attraction of serving cold beer and being situated across the street from Station 59, where Priscilla would be working. Just knowing she was that close would increase the torture and maybe get it out of his system quicker.

Brady's Tavern and Tearoom was on the historic register and had been run by the same family for close to a hundred years. The current owner was Julie, Tony's wife and the original Brady's great-granddaughter. She'd classed the place up since taking over, making it less dingy and more family-friendly, something that had annoyed some of the cops and firefighters who hung out here.

But Roark still liked it fine. He could come here for a friendly game of darts or shuffleboard and a cold beer. And since Julie had taken over, he could also get something other than soggy microwave nachos to eat.

Tonight he chose a stool at the antique carved wood bar, surprised to find Tony behind it.

"I thought rookies couldn't moonlight," Roark said.

"I'm not moonlighting. Julie doesn't pay me, so this is volunteer work. What can I get you?"

"A cold Shiner Bock and a hot cheeseburger, in that order."

"Coming up."

Was it his imagination or was Tony's reception a bit cooler than usual? He wouldn't be surprised. Priscilla was one of Tony's best friends and his landlady. He probably knew about the breakup—and it *was* a breakup at this point. He would be quick to assume the whole thing was Roark's fault.

Roark supposed it was, in a way. If he hadn't made such a big deal about having kids, in such specific terms, maybe Priscilla wouldn't have reacted so strongly. He could have eased her into the idea.

He wanted her back. Priscilla was the missing half that made him whole. It was as simple as that. And while he still believed that children would only enhance their lives, he'd be okay without them.

Unfortunately he would never convince her of that now, not after waxing enthusiastic about swollen bellies and delivery-room cursing and middle-of-the-night feedings.

"I'm surprised to see you're not on duty," Roark said. "Don't you work the C shift with Priscilla?"

"Usually. I traded with someone on A so I could cover for Julie's regular bartender."

"So how's Priscilla?" Roark asked, bracing himself for an angry response. But he needed to know how she was doing. He was like a junkie without his fix.

Tony leveled a look at him. "She's functional."

Well, that told him where he stood in Tony's estimation.

"She wouldn't tell anyone what was wrong, but we all knew it was you."

"Yeah. I'm the jerk, all right." Because he wanted a family.

Tony glared a few moments longer, but then the tension left his face and he just looked more puzzled than anything.

"So what on earth happened?" Tony suddenly demanded. "Everybody thought you guys were perfect together. Priscilla seemed so happy."

"She was happy," Roark said almost to himself. "We were both happy."

"You didn't cheat on her, did you?" Tony looked as though if the answer was yes, he might leap over the bar and throttle Roark. Roark didn't doubt he could do it.

"I didn't do anything," Roark said. "We had a…philosophical difference."

"What does that mean?"

Roark sighed. "It was the whole kid thing."

Tony's hostility immediately returned. "Man, Epperson, I thought you were better than that."

"Excuse me? I'm a criminal because I want kids?"

"No, you're a jerk for rejecting Priscilla for not being able to have kids. How could you be that cruel? That shallow? I never would have believed you'd do something like that. I thought you were—"

"What did you say?"

"I said a lot of stuff. Hey, Julie would kill me if I provoked a fight in here, so let's step outside first if you're thinking about throwing a punch—"

"Of course I'm not going to start a fight. Tony, what did you say a minute ago about Priscilla? You said she isn't *able* to have kids." Not that she doesn't want kids.

Tony looked more confused than ever. "You said it first. You broke up because Priscilla can't have kids."

"Oh, my God."

Tony resumed his rant, but Roark tuned him out. Priscilla couldn't have children? As in, biological impossibility? That would explain her lack of concern over birth control.

And it changed everything.

He thought back to everything he'd said and done having to do with children and babies and he wanted to shoot himself. Dragging her to Boston and immersing her in his nephew's birth, surrounding her with babies and children—what a rough thing to do to a woman with fertility issues.

But he hadn't stopped there. He'd emphasized how much he wanted a big family, going on about family vacations and soccer games….

No wonder she'd reacted so strangely.

"Captain Epperson, are you listening to a word I'm saying?" Tony demanded.

"Just a couple of them," Roark answered, as if the question hadn't been rhetorical. "Did Priscilla's ex-boyfriend dump her because she couldn't have children?"

"I…I don't know. But even if he did, that sure doesn't excuse you for doing the same thing."

"I didn't. Tony, I didn't know."

"Didn't know what?"

"That she couldn't have kids. She told me she didn't *want* kids."

"Oh." Tony's manner changed abruptly. "Well, hell, I probably wasn't supposed to tell you, then."

"The question is, why didn't she tell me the truth in the first place?"

"I have no idea."

But Roark thought he did. He saw it clearly now. Cory had broken up with Priscilla because she couldn't give him children, and she'd thought Roark would do the same thing. So she'd tried to make it easy for him to walk away.

He would have been mad if he didn't hurt so much for her right now.

He pushed his beer aside without ever tasting it. "I have to go straighten this out."

"What about your burger?" Tony said.

"Give it to him." Roark nodded toward a frail old man who was leaning on the bar, looking as if he'd already had a few too many beers.

Roark dropped a twenty on the bar as he stood, ready to do battle.

"You're going to talk to her now?"

"Damn straight."

He nearly ran over a young couple as he exited Brady's, so focused was he on getting across the street to the fire station. Then he almost got run over himself by a pickup truck for the same reason. He didn't feel the cold, didn't notice anything except the fire station's front door.

It was locked, of course. He leaned on the bell until a sleepy-looking Murph McCrae yanked open the door.

"What?" Then he seemed to remember himself. "Evening, Captain." His greeting was glacial.

Roark almost smiled. The veterans might complain a lot about the rookies, razz them and give them the worst possible time. But when the chips were down, the guys were rallying around their own. Priscilla had won some fans among the other firefighters. And how could she not? How could anyone not love her?

He was mad as hell at her right now, but he still loved her so much it was a physical ache in his gut.

"She's here, right?" he asked.

"Upstairs," came McCrae's grudging reply.

Everything downstairs was dark. Murph had watch duty, but no one else was up. Roark made his way through the kitchen to the narrow wooden staircase that led up to the second story. It was dark upstairs, too. With only the glow from streetlights outside and some seismic snoring inside to guide him, Roark found the dormitory. Each firefighter had a cubicle of sorts, defined by a locker and some drawers on one side and a curtained partition on the other.

Most of the bunks were occupied.

At the end of the long row was the glow of a lamp. Roark was betting he knew who was still awake.

Priscilla's was the last cubicle, next to the wall, which afforded her a bit more privacy. The stations were supposed to have separate quarters for women, but 59, one of the city's oldest, didn't exactly meet regulations, and Priscilla hadn't complained.

He peeked around the curtain that shielded her area from curious male eyes. She lay on her stomach on the twin bed, with her head at the wrong end. She was fully clothed except for shoes and she was fast asleep with an open textbook for a pillow.

"Priscilla?" he said softly.

No response.

He entered the space and walked over to the bed, allowing himself a moment to watch her sleep. He loved seeing her face so serene, so free from worry. She looked like an angel. Her caramel-colored hair had come loose from its usual elastic and fanned out all around her.

He sat gingerly on the edge of the bed and lightly rubbed her back, awakening her as he would a dog that just might bite. Not that he and Priscilla had parted in anger, but he was unsure how she would receive him in the middle of the night.

"Priscilla?" he said again as she stirred.

She opened her eyes and rolled onto her back, blinking owlishly. "Roark? What are you doing here?"

"I came to see you."

She checked her watch. "It's after midnight."

"Perfect time for a chat."

She sat up, then stood, putting the bed between them as best she could. "We already said it all, didn't we?"

"Not all. Not by a long shot. Anyway, I thought we were supposed to be thinking about things. We were going to talk again."

She folded her arms and watched him warily. "You have to leave. This doesn't look good."

"I'll leave when I've said my piece."

"All right, then, say it."

"Why didn't you just tell me you *can't* have children?"

Priscilla gasped, then pressed her hand against her mouth. "How did you find out?"

"Does it matter?"

"Tony. That blabbermouth." Then she sighed. "No, I guess it doesn't matter."

"It's true then?"

"Yes. I can't ever get pregnant. Even if I wanted to."

"You should have just told me."

"I couldn't."

He held out his hand to her. "Come here, Pris. Sit down with me. We're going to talk this through, and I want to look at you while we do."

"On the bed?"

"We can go downstairs and sit in chairs if you want. But I'm not leaving until we get a few things settled."

She sank uneasily onto the end of the bed, her logic defeated.

"Now," he said, "did you really think I would break up with you because of this?"

"No." She paused. "Well, at first I was afraid of that."

"Because of Cory?"

"Yeah. I mean, he looked me straight in the eye and said, 'I love you, but I want a wife who can bear my children.' Hearing that once in a lifetime is plenty."

Roark knew only another woman could truly understand how painful that must have been. But he still ached for her. And if he ever ran across this Cory, he would...well, he'd thank the guy for not marrying Priscilla, because she deserved a whole lot better.

"I'm not Cory," Roark said.

"I know. I realize that. You're unselfish and fair and honorable. I knew you wouldn't break up with me. You would stick with me, even if you didn't want to—even if you couldn't stand the thought of going the rest of your life without children—because you're loyal and noble you wouldn't be able to bring yourself to hurt me like Cory did."

He could not believe what he was hearing. "So you think you did me some kind of favor? By letting me believe you didn't want children?" But then an uncomfortable thought occurred to him. "Priscilla, you do want kids, don't you?"

"I've reconciled myself to the fact I won't have any. And I'm okay with that. But you're not."

"You didn't answer my question."

She said nothing, and he let the silence stretch out. "Yes, I want children," she finally answered, her voice barely above a whisper. It felt as if he'd pried the admission out of her. "I've tried to tell myself it isn't so important. I've deliberately avoided putting myself around babies. I tried not to even think about them. But in the end…yeah, I want one."

"Then what's the problem? There are other ways to acquire children besides you getting pregnant."

She stared at him, her eyes growing big.

"I know you've been raised rather conservatively," he said, "but surely you're aware of the options. There are adoption agencies and private adoptions. A zillion babies overseas looking for homes. There are surrogates. We could be foster parents. If we adopted an older child or a special-needs child, we could have one tomorrow."

"Roark, we aren't even married!"

"Is that the only problem?"

Priscilla opened her mouth to reply, but the alarm picked

that moment to go off, nearly jarring them both out of their skins. Bright light filled the upstairs, and a series of groans followed, not the softest of which was Priscilla's.

"Great. Perfect timing. I'm sorry, Roark, but I have to go."

"I know you do."

"Don't move. I'll be back."

"You better come back. You'll be careful, won't you? You know I'm just about ill at the thought of you risking your life."

Her face melted into a smile. "I'm always careful. No stupid fire is going to stop me from coming back, and we *will* continue this discussion exactly where we left off."

"I'm counting on it."

With one final groan, she turned and ran for the pole.

Roark had meant it when he'd said he felt sick. That time he'd been called to a shed fire and had seen Priscilla tromping around on the roof, he'd almost lost his lunch—and he and Priscilla hadn't even been together then.

He knew she was smart and strong and learning from the best. But he still worried. He would always worry.

He hoped he got the opportunity to continue worrying.

Roark decided that waiting on Priscilla's bed did put him on slightly shaky ground. Although wives and girlfriends often visited the station, generally they weren't allowed up here. He tiptoed downstairs, intending to get himself a cup of coffee.

And then his phone rang.

It could only be one of two things, neither of them good. He checked the caller ID. It was the alarm office.

"Captain Epperson? We've got a two-alarm fire at a motel on Ft. Worth Avenue and Kelsey. The first responders say it looks like arson—and it looks like your boy."

He knew, without asking, that this was the fire Priscilla and her crew were heading for. He was already moving toward the door, his keys in his hand.

"I'm on it," Roark said. "I'll be there in five minutes, tops. And I don't care how you do it, but you make sure every person at the scene knows not to go inside. Just let the damn building burn to the ground and stay away from it."

The dispatcher didn't answer. Hell, it wasn't Roark's place to tell whomever the Incident Commander was how to run his fire. But he knew the motel in question. It had been about to fall down even without a fire and it sure as hell wasn't worth saving at the risk of any firefighter's life.

The thought of anything happening to Priscilla because of this sick bastard was unthinkable.

He wouldn't let it happen, even if he had to drag Priscilla away from the fire himself.

Chapter Fifteen

Priscilla hadn't seen a fire like this in months—not since her very first one. They could see the glow two miles away, and when they rounded the corner onto Ft. Worth Avenue and got their first clear view of the flames leaping into the night sky, everyone in her crew gasped.

The motel roof was on fire. There must have been twenty-five or thirty units arranged in a U shape around a parking lot, and the entire roof was blazing as if it had all started at the same time. The sight filled Priscilla with a sense of foreboding.

They all leaped to the ground almost before the engine had stopped, eager to get their assignments. Murph conferred briefly with the Incident Commander from Station 42, then turned back to his people.

"Tate, Garner, you're on search-and-rescue detail," Murph informed them, his voice elevated but calm. "Start at the west end and work your way around. No one seems to know how many people might still be inside, if any."

Some people, at least, had woken up and fled. Several of them stood in the street just beyond the trucks and engines and squad cars, barefoot, blankets wrapped around them, staring glassy-eyed at the spectacle.

"C'mon, Ice Princess," Tate said as he grabbed an ax and a pike pole from the ladder truck that had parked behind them. "Get a ram and shake a leg."

Priscilla grabbed her tools, wishing like hell Otis hadn't chosen today of all days to be home with the flu. Bing Tate just loved being in a position to boss her around. And though he was an experienced firefighter, she knew someday that inflated ego of his would get him in trouble—and possibly her, too.

Just as they were heading for the west end of the motel, pulling on their hoods and breathing apparatuses, Ethan ran up to them. "Wait! We just heard—it's definitely arson. Watch for booby traps."

"It's not the serial arsonist," Bing said confidently. "He's never set fire to an occupied building before."

"Just be careful."

"You, too." Priscilla punched Ethan on the arm, pulled her mask on and headed for the first door. The flames on the roof shot up thirty feet, and the heat was awesome even through all her protective gear. But heat and smoke rise, so it was conceivable people could still be inside, asleep and oblivious.

She didn't bother knocking. She bashed her small battering ram through the lone window and ripped the inside curtains aside. "Hello! Anyone in here?" She shone her flashlight into the small, barren room. It didn't have a stick of furniture in it and it looked deserted.

Bing was already repeating her actions with the second room, so she moved to the third. They kept their eyes on each other; neither would enter the building without the other.

When she broke the window on this unit, smoke poured through the opening. "Hello!" she called out again. "Anyone in here?" Then she thought to repeat her question in

Spanish. Though she didn't have any real knowledge of the language, she'd learned a few key phrases.

This time her flashlight barely penetrated through the smoke. There appeared to be rumpled sheets on the bed, though no one was in it. She would have to go in to make sure the room was truly empty.

"Bing! I'm going in!"

Bing joined her and helped her bash the door open. It gave far too easily; she wondered just how secure the motel's occupants actually believed they were. Knowing the roof was blazing, she glanced up at the ceiling. So far, it looked solid.

"You think someone's in here?" Bing asked dubiously.

"I don't know, but…" Then she heard it. A child's cry for help. "The bathroom!"

Bing pushed ahead of her, racing toward the terrified voice. Priscilla moved in right behind him.

The bathroom door was slightly ajar. Some mysterious instinct made Priscilla shine her flashlight beam to the top of the door. She saw something that didn't look right.

"Bing, no!"

But she was half a second too late. As he pushed the door open, a mountain of bricks fell on his head, knocking him to the ground. At almost the same moment, the ceiling near the door to the outside collapsed.

"Mayday, mayday!" Priscilla shouted into her radio. "I have a man down and I need some water now!" She dragged Bing's unconscious body out of the bathroom doorway and shone her flashlight into the bathroom where the piteous cries continued unabated.

But there was no child in the bathroom. Instead Priscilla saw a boom box.

"I have a man down." Priscilla continued her monologue as she rolled Bing onto his back and pulled him upright. Oh, God, what if his neck was broken? She couldn't even tell if he was breathing. "I'm in the third room from the west end, where the—"

She heard something groaning and cracking overhead. She couldn't wait for water.

Somehow she heaved Bing Tate over her shoulder, grateful now that it wasn't Otis, who outweighed Bing by a hundred pounds. She climbed over the bed, then literally ran through a curtain of fire to the window. She dumped Bing through the opening, then rolled through herself—and got hit with a powerful stream from a hose.

"You're a little late!" she sputtered as a horde of beige coats converged on Bing and then her, dragging them away from the burning building and all the way out to the street, which was completely barricaded. Dozens of people had gathered to watch.

They transferred Bing to a gurney and took him to one ambulance, then tried to lead Priscilla to another, but she refused. She had to see if he was okay. Much as he irritated her, he was still one of her brothers.

"Will you stand still for one second?"

It took her a few moments to realize that one of those beige coats was attached to someone she hadn't expected to see here.

She jerked her mask off. "Roark?"

"God Almighty, woman, you almost gave me a heart attack." He threw his arms around her, and she was warmed by his concern but acutely aware of their audience.

"Roark, we have jobs to do!"

"Not you. You're done for the night."

"There might be more people—"

"The rest of the building has been cleared. And you've got a helluva burn on your face. You're not going anywhere except to the hospital."

Now that he mentioned it, her right cheek did smart. She'd probably knocked her mask askew when she'd heaved Bing over her shoulder, leaving a sliver of exposed flesh. "I'm fine," she said. "Roark, it's the arsonist. The room was booby-trapped." And she recounted her experience with the faked cries for help and the bricks. "What if there's another bomb?"

"We've already cleared the area. You and Tate were the only ones inside."

Bing. The ambulance they'd put him in was already moving, taking him to the hospital.

The IC ordered an aerial brought in to dump water on the fire from above, with all personnel a safe distance away. But the motel was still a total loss.

Priscilla consented to let a paramedic check her out; as her adrenaline dissipated, she realized she hadn't come through the ordeal quite as unscathed as she'd thought. The burn on her face was a long crescent-shaped blister, almost an inch wide at the center; she'd also landed on her elbow when she'd rolled out the window, and now it had swelled to the size of an orange. Various other aches and pains told her she'd probably strained a couple of muscles lifting two hundred pounds of Bing and his gear and sprinting with him across an obstacle course.

As soon as Roark was convinced there were no life-threatening injuries, he went to do his job. Priscilla picked up her gear, which she'd stripped off earlier, and stowed it in the jump seat of Engine 59. She'd lost her battering ram, ax and flashlight and she felt a bit aimless. She was used to dogging Otis's steps and now she was alone.

Then she saw something that caused her to lose her melancholy instantly: a young man in a brown jacket. Though he wore a knit cap instead of the Blue-Lighter cap, he looked disturbingly familiar.

Was it him? Was it Gregory Falen?

He was in the center of a knot of milling people, and she couldn't get a good look at his face. But she didn't want to get closer because he might recognize her. He'd seen her videotaping him that night after Marisa's wedding.

She found Roark.

He was all business, conferring with his team members, who'd been hauled out of bed to help out. They couldn't go into the smoldering motel until the bomb squad had made sure it was free of explosives, but they were mapping out a plan of attack.

His face softened when he saw her. "Priscilla." Just the way he said her name conveyed a zillion emotions, none of which could be explored at the moment.

She drew him aside. "Roark. I think our friend is here again. Gregory Falen."

"Where?" His gaze darted around, searching.

"Over there." She tried to nod nonchalantly in the right direction. "Next to a woman in a red coat. I'm not sure, but I think—"

"Stay here," Roark barked.

He set off toward the crowd of onlookers, his stride angry. He'd hated the arsonist before, but tonight the guy had made it personal. He'd almost killed the woman Roark loved. Still, Roark slowed down so as not to draw attention to himself.

The guy Priscilla had pointed to had separated from the crowd and now stood alone, still staring at the burning motel as if in a hypnotic trance. Roark circled around and approached from behind. He put a hand on the suspect's upper arm, startling him. "I'd like to have a word with you," Roark said, close to the guy's ear. "Come with me." Maybe he didn't have enough probable cause to throw the guy down on the ground and arrest him, but he had enough to stick him in the back of a squad car and have a little chat.

The guy's reaction was fast. He elbowed Roark hard in the ribs, driving the breath out of him, and pulled free of his grip. Then he took off running. Without a moment's hesitation, Roark took off after him. But the younger man was fast, and Roark was hampered by his heavy turnout coat. The suspect darted into the first alley he saw.

Suddenly Roark realized someone was running beside him. "Priscilla! What are you doing?"

"This alley dead-ends at the post office." She squinted after the fleeing man. "We might get him yet."

"How do you know that?"

"Are you kidding? I've got this whole area memorized."

"He could be armed," Roark said, physically slowing Priscilla down. "I can't be responsible—"

"Roark," she whispered. "There he is."

The guy was climbing the chain-link fence that surrounded a post office parking lot. He probably wasn't armed, or he'd have shot at them by now. He certainly didn't have any compunction about killing firefighters—and Roark looked an awful lot like a firefighter at the moment.

Razor wire topped the fence, so the guy was not going to get over without some major bodily damage. Unfortunately Roark had no way of calling for backup unless he used the cell phone in his pocket. This probably wasn't the smartest move he'd ever made. But his judgment had been clouded by fury. Bing Tate might be dead. Roark wasn't going to let this guy hurt one more person.

"Stay back," he told Priscilla. His best chance was to get the guy while his hands were occupied. The suspect had managed to grab on to the branch of a tree. If he could use it for support, he would be able to climb over the razor wire with his feet, suffering minimal damage.

Roark wasn't going to let that happen. He turned on the steam and hit the fence just as Falen got a foothold on the top bar. Roark leaped up and grabbed the guy's shoe, which came off in his hands, and Roark thought for a moment he'd lost his quarry.

Seconds later, though, the suspect fell—right on top of Roark. They landed on the gravel pavement in a heap of tangled legs and flailing arms.

"Don't move or I'll tear your freaking arm off."

"Priscilla?"

The suspect groaned. "Aw, man, get her off of me."

THREE HOURS LATER, Gregory Falen, aka. Douglas Spalding, confessed to the eight arson cases Roark knew about, plus two more that were a surprise. When confronted with the fact that investigators had found gasoline on his clothes and empty gas cans in the trunk of his car, he'd finally caved and had gone from denial to grudging admission. Eventually he worked his way to bragging and finally raving like a lunatic about how his application to the fire department had been rejected on racial grounds because he was a space alien. The guy was probably hoping to get himself off with an insanity plea—or maybe he really was crazy. Roark didn't give a flip so long as he stayed off the street.

As soon as Roark had a signed confession, he left the details to his team. He was bruised and scraped and tired as a dog, and all he wanted was a hot shower and a warm bed.

No, wait, that was all wrong. First, he wanted Priscilla. Her shift was long over. She was probably home catching her own well-earned z's. Roark didn't care. He was going to find her and finish the conversation they'd started at the station before the alarm.

He called her on his cell as he drove across the river back to Oak Cliff, but he got her machine. Maybe she'd turned off the ringer; he knew she did that sometimes because her mother had a habit of calling at ungodly hours.

When he pulled up to her house, though, he didn't see her car, and his heart sank. Where was she? She didn't answer her cell phone either. Should he wait? It seemed wrong to just head home and go to sleep when his entire future hung in the balance.

He was staring at Priscilla's house so intently he didn't realize someone had approached his car until he heard the knock on his window. Startled, he turned to see Ethan Basque standing there, looking a little rumpled and worse for wear. He'd probably been up all night, too.

Roark lowered his window.

"I came outside to get the paper and saw your car," Ethan said, his tone slightly huffy. "Priscilla's not home. She's at the hospital."

"What?" Had she been hurt worse than he realized?

"She's fine, don't worry. She went to see Bing Tate. When he regained consciousness, he asked for her. And she went, of course. The guy did nothing but torment her for months, but in the end he's still one of us." Ethan hesitated, then asked, "You want to come in and have a cup of coffee while you wait for her? You look like you could use one."

Roark had no doubt about that. But he was too antsy to wait around. "Thanks, but I think I'll try to catch up with her." And maybe, just maybe, if they got everything straightened out, they could sleep off their exhaustion in the same bed.

BING LOOKED AWFUL. He had two black eyes from the concussion and he was in traction, with a brace around his neck. But his injuries weren't as serious as everyone had feared. He'd compressed a couple of vertebrae, but nothing was broken.

He appeared to be asleep when Priscilla quietly entered his room, but then he opened his eyes. "Hey."

"Hey, yourself," she said. "Some guys will do anything for attention." Then she paused. Their previous animosity toward each other didn't seem appropriate anymore. "Seriously, how ya feeling?"

"I've been better. But I'm alive. Thanks to you."

Priscilla didn't quite know how to cope with humble gratitude from Bing. "Murph and Ethan were there with the water," she said. "They'd have gotten to us in another few seconds." In truth, Priscilla didn't remember much about what had happened. She remembered seeing the load of bricks a fraction of a second too late to issue a warning. She remembered seeing Bing fall and spotting the boom box. But the moments after that were a blur.

"You know what they're calling you, right?" Bing said. "Super Priscilla. Suprilla. You carry a fellow firefighter out of a burning building, then run down and tackle the arsonist. Are you trying to make the rest of us look bad?" But there was no malice in the question.

"Suprilla sounds like an artificial sweetener, but I guess it's better than Ice Princess." But she really didn't want to be singled out. She and Bing might have had their differences, but he'd have done the same for her. She just wanted to be one of the gang. "I should be the one thanking you. You're the one who insisted on going first into that bathroom."

"That's hardly heroic. You know why I did that, right?"

"Yeah. 'Cause I'm a girl and you're macho, and you were trying to protect me."

"Wrong. I pushed ahead because *I* wanted to be the one to rescue a child. I wanted everyone to call me Mr. Rescue, like they did Ethan when he saved Kat and Samantha."

She was surprised by Bing's frankness. "It doesn't matter why you did it. If you hadn't gone ahead of me, I'd be the one in this bed." Or at the morgue.

"Well, anyway, I just wanted you to know that I'm sorry for the way I've acted. For a long time I didn't think women belonged in the fire service. I didn't think they were strong enough or brave enough. But you've proved me wrong— in a way I'm not likely to forget, ever. So from now on, anyone gives you trouble, you send 'em to me."

Priscilla smiled. She suspected Bing would never completely swear off teasing her. But she didn't think it would bother her anymore.

Someone tapped on the door. "Anyone home?"

"Roark!" She was on him like iron filings on a magnet, throwing herself into his arms almost before he could enter the room. "What happened? Were you able to hold Falen?" It had occurred to her, after cops had dragged the guy away in cuffs, that he'd done nothing wrong except flee. Unless they could find a way to charge him with arson, they'd have had to let him go.

"We did better than hold him," Roark said. "We got a full confession out of him. Ironclad, videotaped."

"God, what a relief," Bing said. "Good work, Captain."

"I had some help. You doin' okay, Tate?"

"I'll be back on duty before anyone even misses me." Priscilla patted his leg. "You need anything?"

He lowered his voice. "How 'bout an Egg McMuffin? You wouldn't believe what they served for breakfast here."

Priscilla laughed. "I'll see what I can do."

She stepped out so that Roark could ask Bing a few questions about what he remembered from the night before, while his memories were still fresh. But she waited in the hall, and a few minutes later Roark joined her.

"You look like a bad stretch of road," she said cheerfully, touching the stubble on his face.

"So do you."

"I've at least had a shower. You still smell like smoke."

"I didn't want to take time for a shower. If you'll recall, we still have some unfinished business."

He sure had that right. If she recalled, their conversation had stopped right in the middle of discussing marriage and children, not in that order.

She punched the elevator button. "Let's go get Bing his breakfast. Then we can talk." And maybe she could pull her thoughts together. Right now they were curling every which way.

Roark waited until the elevator doors closed. "Bing can wait. I don't want to propose marriage in the middle of McDonald's."

Priscilla took one short, panicked breath. "But a hospital elevator is okay?" She'd pictured this moment a little differently.

"It's not ideal. But this can't wait. Priscilla, I want to spend the rest of my life with you. If we can adopt children, that would be wonderful. But if we can't or we decide not to, that's okay, too. Because you are all the family I need. You're what I've been waiting all these years for. If you love me, that's the only thing in the world I'll ever need."

Priscilla wanted to say something, but her throat had closed and no words would come out.

Roark took both of her hands in his. "So, Priscilla Garner, will you marry me?"

The elevator car reached the first floor and the doors opened, but Roark pushed the close button. "Well?"

Priscilla nodded. "But I do want kids. Maybe a whole bunch, I don't know. Maybe we can adopt siblings—you know, the kind that are hard to place because there's more than one and they want to stay together?"

Roark laughed and drew her into his arms as the doors opened again. "Maybe first we should focus on surviving the three-ring circus of a wedding your mother will want to throw. Then we can think about kids."

"Deal." And she kissed him, long and hard and in full view of three elderly women who were not at all sure they wanted to get on the elevator. "Just wait until Marisa sees the bridesmaid dress I pick out for her!"

Epilogue

After more than a year of dickering and speech-making and fund-raising, the firefighters' memorial was finally ready for its dedication. So on a hot, bright Saturday in May, every off-duty firefighter in Dallas—and maybe on the planet, judging from the size of the crowd gathering on a downtown street—came to honor their fallen brethren.

The artist had been working in secret for months, the component pieces of the memorial brought in only the previous week and fitted together like a jigsaw puzzle beneath a tent.

Denny Young, Dallas's charismatic fire chief, took the microphone first; he spoke of bravery and valor and respect and solidarity. Then Murphy McCrae, who'd known and worked with all three fallen men, spoke of friendship and the smaller things that had made up the firefighters' daily lives. He mentioned John Simon's kindness to his dog, Daisy, and David Latier's penchant for cooking hot, hot chili and Lamar Burkins's love of a good practical joke. By the time John Simon's widow spoke a few words of gratitude for the support of the firefighting community, there wasn't a dry eye anywhere.

Finally the memorial was unveiled. It wasn't anything earth-shattering, just a statue of three men in their turn-out gear, carved from a dark brown stone that looked like marble. The men had their arms around each other and smiles on their faces.

The artist had chosen to portray the men as they'd lived, not as they'd died.

Next to the statue was a small fountain with three spigots in cast brass; if one looked closely, the spigots were in the shape of fire hose nozzles. The fountain created a mist, into which the three figures seemed to be walking.

When bagpipes started up, haunting and mournful, the crowd grew silent and even the birds stopped chirping.

And then it was over, and that chapter was closed. The crowd was quiet as it dispersed.

Priscilla, in her dress uniform, somehow managed to find Roark.

He didn't say anything, he just took her hand and squeezed it. She knew he worried about her, but stoically he never mentioned it anymore. "Are you going straight home?" he asked. Though their official wedding wasn't for another month—because her mother had insisted she needed that long to plan it—they'd moved into a big house in Kessler Park, Oak Cliff's fanciest neighborhood. Roark had argued that if they were planning to have all those kids someday—and they were—they might as well start by buying the house they would need.

"I'm stopping at home only to change clothes," she said. "Then I have a little, er, errand to run. Might take me an hour or two."

"How about if I meet you later at Brady's for a burger, then?" Roark gave her a knowing wink.

"Perfect." He obviously knew exactly what she was up to. She, Ethan, and Tony had another little ceremony to attend, just the three of them.

AN HOUR LATER, PRISCILLA and her two best friends—well, best friends besides her husband-to-be—clinked their beer mugs together at Brady's Tavern and Tearoom.

"To our rookie year," Ethan said.

"And thank God it's over," Tony added.

Priscilla shook her head. "Hey, it wasn't that bad." Well, okay, some of it had been really bad. Ethan had been injured during a July Fourth fire last year; then there was the whole serial arsonist thing and the fact that they'd been assigned to every horrible chore Captain Campeon could think of. They'd been ignored and harassed. They'd made mistakes and gotten yelled at.

But they had also proved themselves. They'd stayed the course. And Station 59 had a new rookie, one Dale Krebbs, who was now the butt of everyone's jokes. The way Otis tormented the poor kid made what he'd done to Priscilla look like a ride on a Ferris wheel.

"There was some good stuff, too," Ethan said. "You have to admit our social lives have improved."

That observation earned another toast.

They spent an hour remembering the highs and lows—the grueling paramedic training, which was now in its final months; rescuing a kitten from a fire and trying to keep it a secret from Murph McCrae; Priscilla's more memorable cooking fiascos. They focused mostly on the small moments, though, the ones that made up their lives.

And when they were sufficiently tipsy and maudlin,

they all joined hands. "You guys are my best friends, forever and always," Priscilla said.

"Forever and always," Ethan and Tony echoed.

Roark, Julie and Kat joined them, and it was one of the sweetest nights Priscilla could ever remember. They drank and ate, played shuffleboard and laughed until Priscilla's stomach hurt. Later, she and Roark went home and made love, then simply held each other, talking in soft voices about the future.

Priscilla knew she was the luckiest person on earth.

* * * * *

Turn the page for a sneak preview of
IF I'D NEVER KNOWN YOUR LOVE
by
Georgia Bockoven

From the brand-new series
Harlequin Everlasting Love
Every great love has a story to tell. ™

One year, five months and four days missing

There's no way for you to know this, Evan, but I haven't written to you for a few months. Actually, it's been almost a year. I had a hard time picking up a pen once more after we paid the second ransom and then received a letter saying it wasn't enough. I was so sure you were coming home that I took the kids along to Bogotá so they could fly home with you and me, something I swore I'd never do. I've fallen in love with Colombia and the people who've opened their hearts to me. But fear is a constant companion when I'm there. I won't ever expose our children to that kind of danger again.

I'm at a loss over what to do anymore, Evan. I've begged and pleaded and thrown temper tantrums with every official I can corner both here and at home. They've been incredibly tolerant and understanding, but in the end as ineffectual as the rest of us.

I try to imagine what your life is like now, what you do every day, what you're wearing, what you eat. I want to believe that the people who have you are misguided yet kind, that they treat you well. It's how I survive day to day. To think of you being mistreated hurts too much. If I picture you locked away somewhere and suffering, a weight descends on me that makes it almost impossible to get out of bed in the morning.

Your captors surely know you by now. They have to recognize what a good man you are. I imagine you working with their children, telling them that you have children, too, showing them the pictures you carry in your wallet. Can't the men who have you understand how much your children miss you? How can it not matter to them?

How can they keep you away from us all this time? Over and over, we've done what they asked. Are they oblivious to the depth of their cruelty? What kind of people are they that they don't care?

I used to keep a calendar beside our bed next to the peach rose you picked for me before you left. Every night I marked another day, counting how many you'd been gone. I don't do that any longer. I don't want to be reminded of all the days we'll never get back.

When I can't sleep at night, I tell you about my day. I imagine you hearing me and smiling over the details that make up my life now. I never tell you how defeated I feel at moments or how hard I work to hide it from everyone for fear they will see it as a reason to stop believing you are coming home to us.

And I couldn't tell you about the lump I found in my breast and how difficult it was going through all the tests without you here to lean on. The lump was benign— the process reaching that diagnosis utterly terrifying. I couldn't stop thinking about what would happen to Shelly and Jason if something happened to me.

We need you to come home.

I'm worn down with missing you.

I'm going to read this tomorrow and will probably tear it up or burn it in the fireplace. I don't want you to get the idea I ever doubted what I was doing to free you or thought the work a burden. I would gladly spend the rest of my life at it, even if, in the end, we only had one day together.

You are my life, Evan.

I will love you forever.

* * * * *

Don't miss this deeply moving
Harlequin Everlasting Love story
about a woman's struggle to bring back
her kidnapped husband from Colombia
and her turmoil over whether to let go,
finally, and welcome another man into her life.
IF I'D NEVER KNOWN YOUR LOVE
by Georgia Bockoven
is available March 27, 2007.

And also look for
THE NIGHT WE MET
by Tara Taylor Quinn,
a story about finding love
when you least expect it.

presents a brand-new trilogy by

PATRICIA THAYER

Rocky Mountain
B R I D E S

Three sisters come home to wed.

In April don't miss
Raising the Rancher's Family,

followed by

The Sheriff's Pregnant Wife,

on sale May 2007,

and

A Mother for the Tycoon's Child,

on sale June 2007.

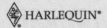

REQUEST YOUR FREE BOOKS!

2 FREE NOVELS PLUS 2
FREE GIFTS!

American **ROMANCE®**

Heart, Home & Happiness!

YES! Please send me 2 FREE Harlequin American Romance® novels and my 2 FREE gifts. After receiving them, if I don't wish to receive any more books, I can return the shipping statement marked "cancel." If I don't cancel, I will receive 4 brand-new novels every month and be billed just $4.24 per book in the U.S., or $4.99 per book in Canada, plus 25¢ shipping and handling per book and applicable taxes, if any*. That's a savings of close to 15% off the cover price! I understand that accepting the 2 free books and gifts places me under no obligation to buy anything. I can always return a shipment and cancel at any time. Even if I never buy another book from Harlequin, the two free books and gifts are mine to keep forever.

154 HDN EEZK   354 HDN EEZV

Name _____ (PLEASE PRINT)

Address _____ Apt. #

City _____ State/Prov. _____ Zip/Postal Code

Signature (if under 18, a parent or guardian must sign)

Mail to the **Harlequin Reader Service®**:
IN U.S.A.: P.O. Box 1867, Buffalo, NY 14240-1867
IN CANADA: P.O. Box 609, Fort Erie, Ontario L2A 5X3

Not valid to current Harlequin American Romance subscribers.

Want to try two free books from another line?
Call 1-800-873-8635 or visit www.morefreebooks.com.

* Terms and prices subject to change without notice. NY residents add applicable sales tax. Canadian residents will be charged applicable provincial taxes and GST. This offer is limited to one order per household. All orders subject to approval. Credit or debit balances in a customer's account(s) may be offset by any other outstanding balance owed by or to the customer. Please allow 4 to 6 weeks for delivery.

Your Privacy: Harlequin is committed to protecting your privacy. Our Privacy Policy is available online at www.eHarlequin.com or upon request from the Reader Service. From time to time we make our lists of customers available to reputable firms who may have a product or service of interest to you. If you would prefer we not share your name and address, please check here. ☐

HAR07

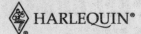

HARLEQUIN®

American ROMANCE®

COMING NEXT MONTH

#1157 FROM TEXAS, WITH LOVE by Cathy Gillen Thacker
The McCabes: Next Generation
Will McCabe arrives in New York City with specific instructions—bring
Samantha Holmes back to Laramie, Texas, for her estranged brother's wedding.
Convincing the fiery brunette to come back with him is one thing.... But Will
realizes he wants her to stay in Laramie for good—and convincing her to do
that is another thing altogether.

#1158 NINE MONTHS' NOTICE by Michele Dunaway
American Beauties
After waiting two years for her perfect man to commit, Tori Adams has decided it's
time to move on. She wants it all—marriage, family, career—and if Jeff Wright
isn't interested, then neither is she! But when Tori discovers she's pregnant, will
nine months' notice change his mind?

#1159 IT HAPPENED ONE WEDDING by Ann Roth
To Wed, or Not To Wed
After the cancellation of her own nuptials a year ago, events planner
Cammie Yarnell avoids planning weddings at the Oceanside B & B. But now a
dear friend wants to get married there and Cammie can't refuse to help, even
though it means working with Curt Blanco—her ex-fiancé's best friend, and the
man who helped ruin her wedding plans!

#1160 THE RIGHT TWIN by Laura Marie Altom
Times Two
Impersonating her twin sister for a weekend should be a piece of cake for
Sarah Connelly. What could go wrong? Running a successful inn isn't as easy
as she thought it would be, though, especially when she falls for a sexy guest!
Heath Brown is perfect for her, but what Sarah doesn't realize is that Heath has
a few secrets of his own....

www.eHarlequin.com

HARCNM0307